"A fascinating, fun and intriguing twist to a story for youngsters. The hero comes through in 'battling' a nefarious dragon while encountering various challenges faced in this tale."

Glenda Prather

"What a great children's book! I picked up "Sir Knight" to read a few pages thinking it would not hold my interest. Much to my surprise, I read the entire book before putting it down. I loved the story."

Judy Wallace

The Adventures of Christian and his unusual pal Winger will delight the minds of children. This tale is a fast page turner and will keep the reader deeply engrossed in the ever challenging events that occur. Each chapter leaves the reader quickly turning the page to find out what is going to happen next. A well written epic tale for children of all ages.

Dr. Carol Foster, Ed.D
Early childhood education

THE ADVENTURES OF SIR KNIGHT

By Louis De Martinis

The Adventures of Sir Knight
Published by Yawn's Publishing
198 North Street
Canton, GA 30114
www.yawnsbooks.com

Library of Congress Control Number: 2015936400

ISBN: 978-1-940395-88-3   paperback
       978-1-940395-89-0   eBook

Printed in the United States

This book was written for my young Grandson, Justin Aden, who at the time lived with his parents and younger brother in Paris, France. It was an attempt by his Grandfather, the author, to keep contact with him. He would be sent a chapter every month or so to peak his interest and to remember his Grandfather who missed him and loved him dearly.

The cover was created by Luciana Donatucci my cousin from Scarfa, Italy. The pictures at the head of each chapter were drawn by my Grandson Michael Kopsho of Atlanta, Georgia.

Chapter 1

Once upon a time, a long time ago, there lived a young lad named Christian. He lived in an enchanted forest with his mother and father and a very nice younger brother.

One day while Christian was walking in the forest, he came upon a wise old owl who was sitting on a lower branch of an old oak tree. He noticed that the owl did not fly away as he approached. As he came nearer to the owl, he realized it had a broken wing and couldn't fly. Christian felt very bad for the owl. He gently patted its head, and it looked at him with pleading eyes. He decided he would take the owl home and try to mend its wing. He made a little box out of twigs, and he covered the floor of the box with leaves and straw. He gently lifted it from the branch of the oak tree and placed it in the box. He slowly walked home being very careful not to bump into anything or jostle the box.

As he approached his house, he saw his mother waiting for him at the front door. He excitedly told his mother about finding the owl and how it was hurt and how he wanted to take care of it until it was able to fly again. His mother looked at Christian and then at the owl in the box that Christian had made. She explained to him that owls were meant to be outside, and she thought that it might not be a good idea to bring him indoors. Christian pleaded with his mother and told her that he would be responsible for the owl. He said he would feed it and take care of it. The owl could stay in his bedroom with him. Christian's mother saw how much Christian wanted to keep the owl, so she gave in and told him that he could take it to his room for the time being, but he would have to speak to his father when he came home from the factory where he worked. Christian thanked his mother and immediately carried the box containing the owl upstairs to his bedroom.

Christian very carefully put the box containing the owl on his desk while he pondered where the best place would be to keep the owl safe so that his brother wouldn't bother it. He decided to keep it in the box on top of the desk and move the desk by the window so the owl would be able to look out the window and perhaps see some of his friends flying about outside. In this way he thought the owl wouldn't get homesick and, besides, Christian was going to be his friend and take care of him. As he pushed the desk by the window, he saw his father coming up the walk. After making sure the owl was okay, he started to run downstairs to greet his father and tell him all about the events of the day and about his new friend. Then, all of a sudden, he stopped on the stairs and thought to himself, *"What if daddy won't let me keep the owl???"* Christian continued down the stairs. He was worried that his father wouldn't let him keep the owl. When he got to the front door hallway, his mother was already there talking to his father. Christian wondered if she told him about the owl. When his father saw Christian he gave him a big smile and bent over and kissed him. Christian told his father all about the events of the day and how he had found the owl. He told his father how the owl was hurt and that he intended to take care of the bird. He searched his father's eyes for a sign of what he would say. Finally, his father asked him if he had named it. Christian hadn't thought about that; he had been too busy worrying about what his parents would do. He asked his father if that meant that he could keep the owl. His father smiled and told him he could if he would promise to take good care of it. Christian was so happy that he jumped up on his father and mother. He kissed them, hugged them, and thanked them.

Christian quickly ran upstairs and told the owl that he could stay. He thought to himself, *"This is silly telling an owl he can stay; he can't understand what I'm saying"*. But the owl let out a soft hoot and looked at Christian as if he understood everything.

Christian began to think of a name for the owl. He wanted a name that would describe the owl and yet be easy to say. The owl was nice looking but he didn't want to call it pretty or handsome. How about the name "Feathers", he thought. No, it just doesn't fit him. Then he began to think of how he found the owl and his sad eyes and broken wing. Then it struck him. *"I'll call him Winger,"* he thought. Yes, it fits him to a tee. He looked at the owl, and it seemed to understand and agree that Winger was a fine name.

Later on, at the dinner table, he told his mother and father and even his little brother that he decided to call the owl Winger. They all agreed that it was a fine name and that it suited the owl. Then his father asked Christian if he had any ideas on how he would repair Winger's broken wing. In all the excitement, Christian hadn't given it much thought. He told his father that he had not. His father suggested that since tomorrow was Saturday and he was not working in the chariot factory, perhaps they could go to town and ask the wizard the best way to help Winger. His father warned him, however, that Winger's condition might be too bad for him to be healed. If that was the case, Winger would probably have to be put to sleep. "No, no, Christian cried, I know he'll be alright, I just know it."

That night, Christian couldn't fall asleep. He was very worried about Winger. He kept tossing and turning until his mother came into his room to see what the matter was. After Christian explained, she told him that there wasn't much they could do about it and that it was in God's hands and all Christian could do was pray. Christian said his prayers and, at last, fell asleep.

Chapter 2

The next morning, Christian felt his father shaking him and telling him to wake up. Christian said good morning to his father and sat up in bed. His father asked him if he had forgotten that today they were going to take Winger to see the wizard. Christian replied that he had not and that he would be ready right away. He looked over at Winger, who was watching him. He quickly jumped out of bed and put on his clothes. He washed up and then proceeded downstairs where his mother had his breakfast waiting for him. He kissed her and said good morning. He then sat down with his father and mother and ate breakfast. While he was eating, he couldn't get Winger out of his mind. Finally, he asked his father if they could go see the wizard right after breakfast, and his father told him that it would be okay. He asked Christian how he was going to carry Winger to the wizard. Christian hadn't thought about that but quickly came up with a solution. He had saved the nest he made to bring Winger home from the enchanted forest. He would use that. His father agreed. Right after breakfast, Christian ran upstairs and got the nest. He went over to Winger and put him on his shoulder so that he could watch everything Christian was doing. He arranged the nest and made it a little more comfortable by placing a small pillow in it. Then he tried to take Winger off his shoulder to place him in the nest, but Winger wouldn't move and clamped his feet on Christian's shoulder as if to tell Christian he wanted to stay right where he was. "Well it's OK with me if you want to ride on my shoulder all the way to the wizard's cave," Christian said to Winger as they proceeded downstairs to meet his father. When Christian's father saw him with Winger on his shoulder, he laughed and told Christian that he looked like a pirate with a parrot on his shoulder.

It was a beautiful spring day in the enchanted forest. The sun was shining, and there was a gentle breeze blowing. It would be a perfect day, Christian thought, if only Winger could be flying next to us, and I was certain that his wing would be alright. Christian was still very worried.

On the way to the wizard, they passed by many of the merchants selling their wares. Christian always liked to look at the different things that were for sale. Today, however, his mind was on more important things. He felt the excitement well up inside him as they approached the wizard's cave.

As he came close to the cave, he could see bats flying around and smoke coming out of a hole at the top that was used for a chimney. As they entered, a voice that was old and scratchy called out from inside, as if somehow the wizard knew that Christian and his dad were approaching. "You must be the one with the owl, I've been expecting you." Christian was confused. There was no way that anyone from inside of the cave could see them approaching. How did the wizard know it was them? Christian felt his legs wobble under him, and he held very tightly to his father's hand as they entered the cave.

Christian was surprised at how light it was inside. He expected it to be dark and dreary and not lit so brightly. The first thing that Christian saw was a fire in the center over which a huge black pot was sitting. The pot appeared to have some kind of liquid inside it which was boiling away. Christian immediately thought about all the stories he had heard about wizard's boiling all kinds of nasty things like toads and chicken feet to make the witches brew that they used in their magic.

Christian's attention was drawn to the wizard, who seemed to appear from nowhere. The wizard looked like a withered old man dressed in a colorful cloak and wore a pointed hat with all sorts of weird symbols on it. The wizard pointed a knarled finger at Christian causing him to step back as he felt his whole body tremble. "I've been waiting for you and Winger," he said with a high-pitched voice that sounded old and scratchy. Christian was determined not to act like the scared boy that he was, so he tried to look into the wizard's eyes and not flinch. "How did you know our names?" he asked the wizard as soon as he got his courage up. The wizard smiled a crooked smile and replied, "I know everything about you. I've been expecting you and Winger". This puzzled Christian all the more. "Don't you know, Christian, that you have to live your destiny, and it was destiny that brought you here to me. You and Winger have a very important quest to embark upon, and I'm the one who will tell you about it." "Quest? What quest?" Christian and his father asked at the same time. "You have been given a very special mission which will be fraught with danger. If you accept the quest, you will be given extraordinary powers, and if you're successful and survive, you will have the gratitude of an entire country," the wizard screeched. Christian looked at his father, who was standing next to him, with a look of disbelief on his face. "But, but, he's only a boy," his father stammered. "As I said, he will be given extraordinary powers. More than he needs to complete the mission." Christian and his father didn't know what to say, they were so stunned by this unexpected development. Then Christian thought about the reason he had come there in the first place. "How about Winger's broken wing, can you fix that?" Christian asked. "It is already mended," the wizard answered. "He, too, will have extraordinary powers and will help you if you decide to accept the challenge of the quest." "But, I still don't understand," Christian replied. "What do you expect me to do?" The wizard looked deep into Christian's eyes and responded, "I don't expect you to do anything more than your duty. This is what you were born for. There is a nation of children that have been enslaved for many years, and they are about to be murdered by the arch villain Mustgreed. A power greater than mine decided it was time that they be set free. I think your conscience will not allow you to let

8

these children be murdered. Now, come closer, and I will tell what awaits you if you decide to accept the quest to save the children." Christian took a step closer and suddenly realized he was more curious than afraid. The wizard had a look on his face as if he were in deep thought. Then he quickly looked down at Christian and said in a very slow, deliberate voice, "Beyond this village lies a dark and mysterious forest which is filled with dangerous creatures. The village of the children lies beyond this dark forest, so to get there you must first cross through it to the other side. Among the monsters that inhabit the dark forest is a dragon of enormous proportions. He is bigger than a house. It is because of him that no one has ever made it to the opposite side. They say that the dragon can smell a human and that no one can escape its murderous wrath. He breaths fire, flies high into the sky and can attack without warning. He must be destroyed in order to rescue the children. First, however, you must survive the traps and snares he has set up to capture his prey. Then you must evade the other animals and snakes that inhabit the forbidden forest. If you survive all this, you must battle with the gigantic dragon and slay him. Only then will you be able to exit the forest on the other side." The wizard let out a sigh and continued, "If, by some miracle, you make it, you will then have to defeat Mustgreed and his army who are holding the children as slaves, and then you must lead the children back through the dark forest with all its perils to safety."

"How can I do this?" Christian asked. "I'm only seven- years-old and barely big enough to play around with a dog, much less fight a dragon." "I told you I will give you the secret of the power that you have within you. I will also arrange that you will have a powerful sword and a shield that cannot be pierced, along with other weapons and equipment that you may need," the wizard said.

Christian was really confused at this. He didn't have a chance to respond before the wizard held out his hand and uttered some words. A great cloud of smoke appeared on the floor of the cave, and when it cleared a golden shield, sword and lance stood against the far wall. On the shield was a crest, and in the crest were the words **"SIR KNIGHT"**. "But, but," Christian began to stammer, "they're... they're bigger than I am. I won't even be able to lift them". "Accept the quest to save the children, and I will give you the secret to the power, and you will become six feet tall and as strong as ten men. I will give you a companion to accompany you on the quest. The companion will be wise and will give you counsel, as well as being a fierce fighter who will aide you in battle."

Completely flustered, Christian looked at his father and asked him what he should do. His father said that it was up to him. He could not help Christian make the decision because he loved Christian too much, and that would make him want Christian not to go. Christian looked from his father to the wizard and said, "O.K. I've made up my mind. I have decided to accept the challenge." Christian looked to his father for approval, but his father couldn't say anything. He just squeezed Christian's hand a little harder.

"Very well," the wizard said. His voice seemed to become a little softer, "This is what you must do. Tomorrow night there will be a full moon. This is the only time that it is feasible to enter the black forest. First you must go to the church at the edge of the forest and wait in the cemetery behind the church until all the clouds have passed over the moon. When this happens, you will see a path entering into the forest. You must take this path for about a half mile. Whatever you do, do not leave the path for the first half mile.

That part of the forest is full of snares. There may be different enticements to try to get you off the path, but don't be fooled; they are all images of deception to get you to deviate from the path so that you may be trapped. "How will I know when I have gone a half mile?" Christian asked. "There will be two horses waiting in a small clearing at that location. These will be your trusty steeds. They will aid you in your battle with the evil forces that lurk in the black forest. Remember, once you enter the forest, there is no turning back," the Wizard cautioned. "If you have any doubts, you must not enter the forest. There will be no returning until the forces of evil that live there are defeated. Go now and say your goodbyes to your family." "But, I thought you said you were going to give me the secret of the power?" Christian asked. "When the time is right you will have the secrets. Believe me, you will find them for yourself before you enter the forest. Be sure that you have Winger with you and that you are prepared for the most terrible fear you will ever know," the Wizard chided.

Christian and his father left the Wizard and started for home. Christian's mind was spinning with thoughts of what lay before him. How was he going to say goodbye to his mother and father. Would he ever see them again? Did he make a mistake accepting the quest? Would he be able to save the children? He was so engrossed in his thoughts that he did not even notice the market or the people who smiled at him and said hello. His father felt the same way. He was sad that Christian was going to leave him, but he was very proud that he had accepted the quest.

When they arrived home, his mother was sitting in the living room knitting a sweater. He had seen her working on it for so long. She was making it for him. He would get annoyed when she would ask him to stand in front of her while she made measured to make sure that she was making it the right size. It seemed like he had to stand there for hours although he knew it was only minutes. Somehow though, tonight he wished that she would ask him to try the sweater again. As he entered the room, she looked up at him and smiled and said, "Christian, why don't you come here a minute so I can try the sweater on you. It's almost finished." "I have something I have to tell you mom," Christian gulped trying to find the right words.

Chapter 3

Morning seemed to come very slowly. Christian had told his mother last night about the Wizard and the quest. He made sure he didn't say too much about the black forest or what lay ahead of him. His mother seemed to take it rather well. She didn't cry or worse try to talk him out of it. She was obviously upset, but she tried not to show it.

Christian looked over at Winger, who was perched on a clothes pole next to Christian's bed as if to be keeping watch over him. Christian slowly took the few steps over to the window, parted the curtains and looked out. It was a terrible looking day. It was cloudy, and the ground was wet. It looked like it could rain at any minute. Christian thought to himself, *it's about nine hours until it gets dark. I guess I'll head for the church around eight p.m. Maybe I should wait until midnight,* he thought. He quickly dismissed the idea when he realized he wasn't even allowed out at that hour. Maybe my dad can tell me what the best time is to leave.

Christian put on his favorite clothes and went downstairs for breakfast. His father and little brother were already sitting at the breakfast table. His father was drinking coffee, and his brother was playing with his bowl of cereal. His brother ate the same cereal every day; he never tried anything different. Christian was glad his dad was off from work today. Hopefully, they could spend the day together and have some fun. His mother came into the kitchen and, with her usual smile and cheerful tone, said good morning to him and asked what he would like for breakfast. Christian asked for pancakes and his mother started sorting through pans under the kitchen cabinet until she came out with the frying pan and a bowl in which to mix the ingredients. She busied herself preparing the breakfast. Christian loved to watch his mother cook. It was like magic the way she took everything and mixed it all up and then cooked it and made it taste so good.

After breakfast, they went into the living room where they talked, and Christian played games with his little brother for a while. His dad lit a fire in the fireplace even though it really wasn't cold. It made it feel so nice, warm and peaceful. It made Christian sad for a little while thinking about how he was going to leave the people he loved and perhaps never see them again. He hoped he had the courage to carry on; after all, the children on the other side of the black forest didn't have any of this.

Chapter 4

That night, he began walking toward the church with Winger on his shoulder. He had gone up to his brother's room earlier to say goodbye. His brother was sound asleep on his bed. Christian bent over him and kissed him. Funny, he thought, normally he would never want to kiss his little brother, but now he wanted to. He knew he would miss him. He would even miss the arguments they had. He felt closer to him tonight than he ever had before. It really had been tough saying goodbye to his mother and father. He had kissed them and hugged them as hard as he could. He told them how much he loved them and how much he would miss them but assured them that he would be returning soon. They told him that they loved him and would always keep a light in the window for him so that he could find his way home when he returned. He was very grateful that they didn't say anything to discourage him. *Wow*, he thought, *they are the best parents in the whole world.*

Christian's mind snapped back to what was happening. *No time for sentiment or memories now,* he thought. *I've got too much ahead of me.* He realized that the moon was hidden behind the clouds just as the wizard said it would be. It made the night seem very dark and dreary. A shudder went through his body as he thought about going into the cemetery. As he walked through town, he could see lights in the windows of some of the houses. Most people were getting ready for bed, but not Christian.... he was on a quest.

The priest had finished reading his book when he looked up from his easy chair towards the window. Was that the gate to the cemetery? No, it couldn't be, it's so dark out..... No one in their right mind would go into the cemetery on a night like this. He placed his book down and went to the window and stared out. For a second, when the moon came out from behind the clouds, he thought he saw a boy walking in the cemetery. No, it couldn't be. It must be one of the stones. The night is playing tricks on these old eyes of mine, he thought. Just then, a bright light, brighter than any light he had ever seen, was shining into the window temporarily blinding him.

Christian reached for the gate to the cemetery. He looked up and saw the light shining in the priest's window. He tried to open the gate quietly, but it was old and rusty and squeaked loudly as he opened it. He closed it behind him and started to walk in. He was scared. He tried to control his legs, but they felt like they were going to shake off his body. They were like gelatin. He slowly walked into the cemetery, toward the back, in the direction of the dark forest. He looked for the Wizard but didn't see him. He was not surprised because it was so dark out. If it wasn't for the little light coming from the window it would be totally dark. Fear filled Christian's mind. What did I get myself into, he thought. I'm no hero. I can't save anyone. All I want to do is go home and be with my parents and my little brother. Just then a bright light lit up the entire cemetery. Christian quickly raised his hand to shield his eyes, but he saw something in the light. It was...

Chapter 5

The housekeeper in the priest's residence was just preparing to get into bed when the bright light shown through the window. Even the shade did not stop it. She quickly went to the window and pulled up the shade and was immediately blinded by the light. She quickly fell to her knees sure that she was dead. She had heard from many people that had near death experiences that they would see a bright light beckoning them. She thought that perhaps she had had a heart attack and was now seeing the bright light beckoning her on her journey to see God. She frantically started praying.

Downstairs, the priest had a totally different reaction to the light. He lowered his shade and tried to shield his eyes from it. It must be a falling star or something similar he thought.

Meanwhile, Christian saw, in the center of the light, what appeared to be a knight. He wasn't dressed in armor but carried a sword and a shield. The shield had something written on it. Christian strained his eyes to read it. It read St. Michael. Christian felt a sense of peace and calmness come over him, something he hadn't felt since his visit to the wizard. In his concentration on the light, he didn't notice that Winger had flown from his shoulder to the ground next to him. The knight spoke to him in a quiet yet strong voice. "Are you ready to accept the challenge of the quest?" he asked. Christian looked up at him and saw him more clearly, his eyes no longer bothering him. "Yes," he responded with as much vigor as he could manage. "Very well, then kneel before me and receive the blessings of the one who sent me." Christian complied and knelt before the knight who placed his sword on Christian's shoulder and said, "I dub you Sir Knight and charge you with the responsibility to defend all that is good, to rescue those that are held captive, and to live as a knight of old, with honor and virtue". The knight then turned towards Winger and said, "I charge you with the responsibility to render all aid and assistance as may be necessary to assist Sir Knight in his quest". Christian looked up at St. Michael and asked, "What must I do to save the children and to survive the dark forest?" He was surprised at how deep his voice had become. "You must survive by your own wits. There is nothing physically I can do to assist you. You already have the courage to accomplish your mission or you would not have accepted the quest. Have faith in yourself and your abilities. I will try to assist you by sending you messages in many ways you cannot understand now. You face many challenges that are beyond most people's comprehension. You can overcome these challenges by always doing what is right and by staying focused on the quest. I must leave now. Be strong and fear not, because right will always win over the evil that is in the world." With that, St Michael was gone.

Christian noticed that the shield and sword from the wizard's cave was lying at his feet. He also noticed his feet were much bigger, and in fact, he was much bigger. He couldn't believe how big he was, probably over six feet he thought. Then he looked at Winger. Oh no... he couldn't believe what happened to Winger.

Chapter 6

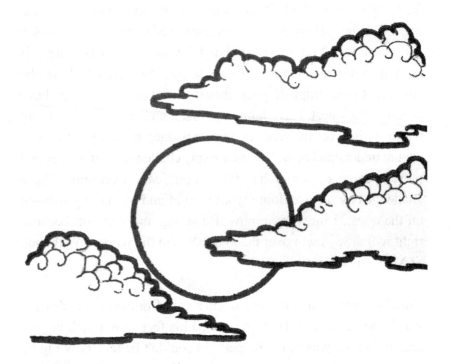

When the bright light disappeared, the housekeeper didn't know whether to be glad or sad. After all, she thought that she was going to be taken up to heaven by the light. Then she thought, maybe I really didn't see the light. It came and went so quickly. Could I have imagined it? She didn't get much sleep that night.

Christian stared at Winger in disbelief. He was standing there on two feet like a man. Standing erect, he was at least six feet tall. His arms and legs had feathers on them, but they were folded in such a way, close to his body, that they really weren't that distinguishable. Instead of hair, he also had feathers that were folded back from his brow to the back of his neck. His face was half man and half owl. His eyes were still the clear eyes of an owl, but his mouth was a small beak. Christian stared at him in awe but wasn't prepared for what happened next. Winger looked at him and **SAID,** "I don't believe this is happening to us". "You...you talked," Christian said. "Yes I did... didn't I?" Winger responded. They must have stood there looking at each other for a good five minutes until Christian realized that the clouds had moved, and the moon was shining brightly, lighting the way to the dark forest. "Quick Winger, while the moon is bright, let's get moving". Christian picked up his sword and strapped it around his waist thinking about how it fit him perfectly when only a few moments ago it as big as he was. He lifted the shield and smiled at how light it was. *Wow,* he thought to himself, *I'm a real man and I must be very strong.* He glanced back at Winger who had a large lance and a shield. On his shield was the same crest as Christian's, but it had a big W in the center where Christians read "Sir Knight". "Quick, no time to waste," Christian said as he leapt over the fence of the cemetery and headed toward the forest with Winger following closely.

They followed the edge of the forest looking for the path to enter. The forest looked pitch black and forbidding. "It should be here somewhere," Christian said. "Don't forget we must not deviate from it no matter what," Winger added. Then all of a sudden, there it was. It was about four feet wide and barely visible. Christian took a deep breath and entered with Winger close behind. As they entered, they noticed that in places the shrubbery had grown over the path making it look like a tunnel. "I don't like the looks of this", Christian said. He was wondering whether he should hack at it with his sword but decided against it and crouched under it. At that point he realized that he could no longer see the outer edge of the forest or the cemetery. They were committed. There was no turning back.

They had traveled about a quarter of a mile. "So far, so good," Christian said. He no sooner got the words out of his mouth when they heard a scream. They were both startled. It was the scream of a little girl. "There she is," Winger said pointing to his right. Christian took out his sword and was about to enter the forest, when Winger yelled, "Look out!" ...but it was too late...

Chapter 7

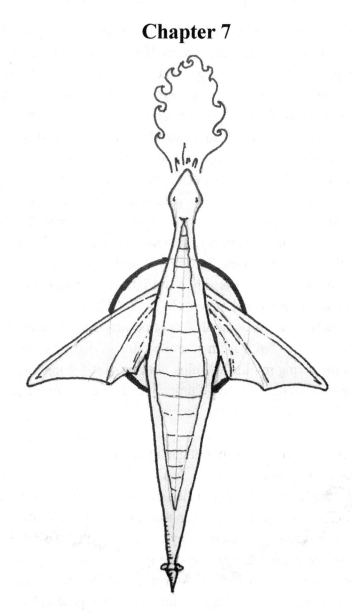

Christian had stepped into the forest in an attempt to rescue what he thought as a little girl in trouble. Winger, remembering the warning of the wizard not to stray from the path for the first half mile, immediately swung into action. He leapt at Christian, pulling him back onto the path, just as spikes attached to vines from the tops of trees slammed down and into the earth. One step further and Christian would have been impaled by one of these spikes. He looked up at Winger who had knocked him over and landed on top of him. Christian smiled and pushed Winger off of him, jumped up and was about to reenter the forest. He knew that the little girl had to be kept there against her will, and she was in trouble, and that he had to try to rescue her. The movement of the spikes from the trees above and the impact when they plunged into the ground, shook the forest and knocked over what he thought was a little girl. It was obvious now; it was only a stuffed doll. Christian looked at Winger in disbelief and anger. He said, "We really have to be careful; whomever is doing this must be very cunning and full of terrible tricks". Christian then smiled and added, "by the way, thanks for saving my life". "Think nothing of it," Winger replied. "I'm sure you'll have plenty of time to repay me before we get out of here".

They continued on the path trying to ignore the terrible sounds and shrieks coming from the forest. Finally they could see a clearing ahead. They cautiously approached the clearing, trying to make as little noise as possible; however the leaves and small branches under foot would give them away to anyone who was listening. Christian bent over keeping his body as low to the ground as possible. Winger took the lead knowing that his sharp eyes were needed to see if any danger lurked in the peaceful-looking clearing. He peeked into the clearing and saw two horses just as the wizard had said. He signaled Christian that it was all clear. Christian took this opportunity to relax a little. He realized that he had been extremely tense and his body ached. He entered the clearing behind Winger and looked around. Nothing suspicious, he thought. Christian asked Winger, who had moved to one of the horses and was patting its head, if he still had the night vision of an owl. Winger told him he did and began to scan the forest in a complete circle. "What do you see?" Christian asked. "I can only see ten or twenty feet into the forest," Winger responded, "It's very dense in there, but it looks quiet". "O.K." Christian said, "I think we'll rest here and wait for the sunrise before we continue". I think we'll be safe here," Winger agreed, "besides the horses will warn us if they hear anything out of the ordinary". They both gathered some leaves in an attempt to fix a makeshift bed for themselves.

Both Christian and Winger were very tired. Christian tried to sleep, but the excitement of all the activity that day kept him tossing and turning. All of a sudden, the sky seemed to be on fire. It turned bright red, and then they heard a roar so loud the ground shook. Without warning it became pitch black, and the horses whinnied and looked as if they were going to run away. Christian jumped to his feet groggy from being awakened from a deep sleep. He immediately grabbed the reins on the horses and tried to quiet them. He looked up but saw only darkness. As his eyes started to get used to the night, he noticed a silhouette in the sky. He turned to Winger and asked, "What is it?" Winger was already staring at the sky with his sharp owl eyes. "It's the dragon," he exclaimed. "It's huge; it must be bigger than a house". Just then, it passed overhead and out of sight, and the clearing was lit by the full moon once again. Christian sat on the ground and looked at Winger. "I guess it's so big that when it flew over it blocked out the moon and that's what made it seem so dark," Winger explained. "What made the sky light up?" Christian asked. "If I were to guess," Winger responded. "I would think that it was spewing out fire." Christian looked at Winger in disbelief. "How are we ever going to get past it or kill it?" he asked, half muttering to himself. "I wish I knew," Winger responded. "I wonder why it didn't just attack us while we were sleeping," Christian continued. "Maybe it didn't see us," Winger answered. "Well, let's keep that in mind. Maybe it can't see at night or, more than likely, it didn't see us because we were beneath it. It made so much noise that it probably didn't hear us either," Christian thought out loud.

They both lay down and tried to go back to sleep, but it was no use. They had their minds on the dragon and how large it was and how they would ever survive a battle with it. Christian knew that if they were going to survive they would have to outsmart the dragon because it was so big that it probably would be impossible to kill.

The dawn broke, and within minutes the sun was shining brightly into the clearing waking up its sleepy occupants. Christian slowly got to his feet, looked over at Winger and then looked at the horses that were leisurely munching on the lush grass of the clearing. He noticed for the first time since he entered the dark forest the sounds of birds singing and animals scurrying about in the underbrush. The cheerful songs of the birds made Christian feel a little better. "There's a stream off to our left," Winger volunteered. They both walked in that direction, leaving a small path in their wake.

The stream was about twenty feet wide and looked to be about two feet deep and was running rapidly on its course. Christian took off his clothes and waded into the deepest part. It felt good to have the water splashing against his body and removing the dirt and grime from the last twenty- four hours. Winger sat next to the shore alternating splashing water on his body and then drinking from his cupped hands. Well, this may not be too bad after all, Christian thought. At least the dark forest seems to have life and....before he could finish his thought, the stream seemed to pick him up and started to carry him away. He tried to make for the shore, but it was no use; the current was too strong and was dragging him under.

Christian lost his balance as the strong current of the stream forced his legs out from underneath him causing him to fall and submerge into the deep part of the stream. He gasped for air but only swallowed water as he couldn't keep his head up and out of the water long enough to catch his breath. Finally, after what seemed to be an eternity, he was able to grab onto a small branch of a tree that was hanging low over the stream as he went speeding by. With the help of the branch, he managed to lift his head out of the water slightly and was able to inhale a few quick breaths. All of a sudden, the small branch broke. He again found himself being mercilessly hurled down the rapidly moving stream. The current increased in speed, and he felt himself being pushed faster and faster down the stream. He felt sharp pains all over his body as the water threw him against the endless numbers of rocks that lined the bottom and sides of the swift running water.

In the meantime, Winger was just about to walk away from the stream when Christian's thrashing caught his eye. He thought for a moment that he might just be playing around and enjoying the cool fresh water. He soon stopped in his tracks when he realized that Christian was not playing and that he was in serious trouble. Winger immediately sprang into action. He tried to run along the shoreline hoping that he could catch up to Christian. He thought that if he could catch up to him he could throw him a branch from one of the trees and haul him out of the water. He soon realized that the trees and shrubbery that had grown next to the stream made it impossible for him to move fast enough to catch up to Christian; who, by this time, was traveling at an enormous rate of speed and was far ahead of him. He had to think fast. It was obvious that Christian was in trouble and needed his help, but what could he do?

Christian continued being carried down the stream at a terrific rate of speed. The water was throwing him from side to side and sometimes flipping him until his feet were out of the water and his head was near the bottom. It was only during this tumbling motion, when his head came to the surface, that he was able to catch a breath. Then it happened. He felt a sharp blow to his head when he hit a rock as he hurdled faster and faster down the stream. He was losing consciousness. I have to fight it, he thought. If I lose control I will certainly drown. It was too late. The blow to his head made him slowly drift into unconsciousness. As he drifted off, he felt as if he were falling asleep. His body felt very light, and he couldn't think or do anything. He had lost control. Then he began having a dream. A weird dream.... a big bird was flying over him, and then, nothing.

Chapter 8

Christian woke up and looked around not knowing where he was. He tried to sit up but was a little dizzy. He lay back down. He could hear the birds singing and felt the sunshine warm against his skin. He lay there for a little while longer and then decided that it was time to get up. He rolled onto his side and lifted himself up on one elbow. He looked around still a little confused and not sure of where exactly he was or how he got there. It was then he realized he was back in the clearing. The two horses were there munching on the fresh grass. As his eyes were able to focus better, he saw that his clothes were hanging over some bushes nearby. Winger was there lying on the ground about ten feet from him. He was sound asleep.

Christian slowly crawled towards Winger. His head was aching where he had bumped it against a rock while being hurled down the river. He was going to wake Winger up but decided against it. He looked so peaceful quietly sleeping. Christian guessed that Winger must be exhausted to be sleeping so soundly in what, apparently, was the middle of the day. Christian looked up at the sun. It was high in the sky, so he calculated that it must be around noon or 1 p.m. He reached up with his hand and started to massage the bump on his head. He suddenly remembered the water and his tumbling over and over and losing consciousness. *How did I get from the water to the clearing,* he wondered? *Winger must have somehow rescued me,* he thought. *I know I didn't make it on my own.*

After a couple of wobbly attempts, Christian was finally able to stand. He slowly walked over to the bushes where his clothes were. After he dressed, he walked over to the horses and began petting them. After a few minutes, he noticed that Winger began to stir. Winger looked over at Christian smiled and slowly got to his feet.

"Well, what happened?" Christian asked.

"You really scared me," Winger answered. "I thought sure you were a goner. I pumped enough water out of you to fill a bathtub,"

Winger chuckled.

"I don't understand. What happened? How did I get here?" Christian asked with a bit of impatience in his voice.

"Well, Winger said, I saw you being dragged down the river and performing some crazy stunts, and I figured you were in trouble. I tried to reach you, but I couldn't. There was too much brush growing along the riverbed, and you were traveling too fast. Next thing I know, I took off".

"I still don't understand," Christian said. "What do you mean you took off?"

"That's it, before I knew it I was flying. It just came naturally to me. I thought that I couldn't fly anymore after I grew so much and became so human, but there I was... flying again. I flew over to you, lifted you out of the water and brought you here. Oh yes, then I had to pump the water out of you, and you were unconscious through the whole thing."

Christian looked at him, in shock, not knowing whether to comment on his flying or his rescue. Finally he said, "I guess I should thank you again for saving my life". Winger looked at Christian and shrugged his shoulders, as if to say that it was nothing.

"You mean you can actually fly, like...like an owl?" Christian said. "Yes, look." Winger spread his arms and the feathers on them extended. He then made a few movements up and down with his arms, and he lifted off the ground. Christian looked on this scene in amazement.

"Then you must have been the big bird flying over me in the water," Christian said. "I thought I was dreaming the whole thing."

They waited a little longer in the clearing until they were sure they felt strong enough and rested enough to start their journey further into the dark forest. While they waited they feasted on berries and fruit that were growing abundantly in the forest around them. Having had their fill, they decided it was time to move on. They saddled the horses and put the armor breast plates on them that they had found in the clearing. The horses were very friendly and gentle and allowed Christian and Winger to fasten the various belts and ties necessary to secure the armor. Then they mounted the horses, and taking their shields and weapons, they moved into the forest along a path that was about four feet wide. Winger took the lead using his sharp eyes to scan the forest as they moved forward. It was dark in the forest even in the early afternoon. The thick foliage and the heavy canopies of the trees blocked out most of the sun, except for an occasional ray, which managed to get through and made the forest seem even more sinister.

At first, Christian would tense at every sound he heard emanating from the heavy, dense wood. After a time, however, he became used to the shrill sounds of the various animals and birds that inhabited that part of the forest.

They had ridden for about two hours when they decided to dismount and take a break. After all, neither one of them was used to riding horses, nor did they want to overdo it on their first day. They walked for a while with their horses slowly following behind each of them at the end of the reins they held. Then, they mounted their steeds and rode for a while and then walked again finding that this routine seemed to be the best way to travel. It was easier on them, and the horses, so they alternated between riding and walking.

Before they knew it, evening started to fall. Although Winger's eyes could see through the darkness of the night, they knew that their horses couldn't, so they decided it was time to make camp. The path they were following had become very narrow and was only wide enough for them to walk through. Christian and Winger decided that, while they still had some light, they would cut a clearing big enough for them to spread out a bit to get some sleep. They pulled out their swords and took wide swings sending bushes and plants flying about. Their sharp swords made quick work of the dense underbrush, and within a short period of time, they had a very respectable clearing wide enough for themselves and their horses with plenty of room left to spare. Christian decided that they should have a fire to keep the wild animals at bay. It would also keep them warm throughout the chilly evening. He gathered up wood, of which the forest yielded a plentiful supply. They started a fire, and with water and some dried vegetables that Christian's mother had packed him, made a soup mixture and cooked it until it was hot and steamy. They savored it as they ate and decided that they already had their fill of fruit that they had foraged. Tomorrow they would see if they could find some nuts and capture some wild game that they could cook and eat.

After their light supper, they made some beds out of whatever soft underbrush they found. Christian gathered more wood for the fire. Some he put on the fire, and the rest he laid alongside for the remainder of the night when the fire would burn itself low. After Winger took a look around and was satisfied that all was quiet, they nestled into their makeshift beds. Still hurting from the problems they had encountered with the stream and still feeling exhausted from their efforts, they almost immediately fell fast asleep.

Neither of them had noticed the large, round, bloodred eyes staring at them from the forest. The large beast stood about seven feet tall. It looked like an alligator or crocodile that stood up on its hind legs. It had a tail like a crocodile with sharp spikes emanating from it. Its body was full of scales that were so hard and closely intertwined that they acted as a shield. It could not breathe fire yet or fly. After all, it was just a small dragon. Someday it would grow up and be as large as a house and rule its own forest. But now, it just waited patiently. Its bloodred eyes moving from the fire to its next feast, which were the two figures lying on leaves peacefully sleeping. Just waiting....waiting for the fire to die out, and then it thought....*they're all mine.*

Chapter 9

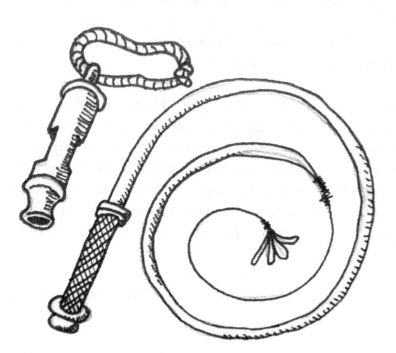

Little Marie was woken by the harsh yelling of one of the drones. "Get up, get up," he yelled, as he snapped his whip against the floor sending a resounding crack which reverberated throughout the hovel where she and twenty other children were sleeping.

"We have work to do. If you work hard today, our exalted leader, Mustgreed, may even give you something to eat." He laughed and snarled at the same time. Marie shivered. Her stomach ached at the thought of food. She had almost nothing to eat yesterday, and the crust of hard bread she received last night for her supper she had shared with Sue, who barely had enough strength left to work. She was very worried about Sue. She knew that whenever someone couldn't work, the drones would come and take them out, and they were never seen again. She didn't want this to happen to Sue. They were friends, and she would miss her terribly. No one knows what happens to the "non-workers", as the drones would call them when they were taken away.

Marie quickly got up and looked over at Sue, who had not moved. Marie then turned her attention back to the drone. It was Nasty. That was the nickname they gave to him. They had named most of the drones. The names usually described their disposition. Marie waited for the drone to turn away. When he was looking in the other direction, she quickly crawled on her hands and knees to where Sue was sleeping. She shook Sue who barely opened her eyes.

"Come on, get up, hurry," Marie said. "We have to get going before he sees us."

"I, I can't. I can't move," Sue responded. "I'm just so tired, please leave me alone."

"You have to get up, or he'll take you away. Come, I'll help you," Marie pleaded.

It took all the strength that Marie could muster to get Sue up on her feet. They staggered as they rose. Marie tried to straighten Sue's torn and tattered dress in an attempt to make her look as if she was okay. She whispered to Sue, "I'll share my food with you. Come, stand straight, you'll be fine. Be careful, he's coming this way".

The drone looked at them and started toward them raising his whip over his head. He looked as if he was about to strike them, but when he swung the whip, it landed at Marie's feet causing her to jump back, and in the process she let go of Sue. Sue immediately slumped back to the ground. The drone looked down at her and slowly said,

"Aha, I see we have a non-worker here. Come with me, I'll take good care of you".

He grabbed her by the arm and started to drag her towards the door when Marie pleaded with him.

"Please," she said. "She'll be alright, you just scared her with the whip and she fainted."

The drone looked down at Sue, and then said to Marie, "I don't think so, and I think she just doesn't want to work. She must be taken away".

"You don't want to do that," Marie pleaded. "She works very hard, and if you took her away, our production will fall off. She is such a hard worker. Mustgreed will not like that."

The drone looked confused. He knew he was responsible for production. At the same time, he had his orders to take away any non-worker.

"I don't see what difference it makes, you will all be taken away soon. You are all worn out and too lazy to work. I'm sure our exalted leader, Mustgreed, will be bringing in replacements soon.

Then you will all be taken care of."

He once again grabbed Sue by the wrist and was dragging her towards the door. Marie was frantic. She couldn't let him take her away. She probably would never see Sue again. Marie picked up a bench and slammed it into the drone. He looked at her in disbelief as he fell to the ground, letting go of Sue's wrist. Marie quickly got Sue to her feet and ran out of the hovel as the drone staggered to his feet looking for his whistle. He started blowing his whistle as loud as he could.

By the time Marie, who was half carrying and half dragging Sue, got outside the door, the whole camp was ringing with the alarm. Marie saw several drones heading her way from their building. She realized that she would never be able to outrun them and carry Sue. She led Sue behind some garbage cans where they hid until the drones ran past them and into the hovel to see what the problem was. As the drones talked to Nasty, Marie lifted Sue and started to lead her to the next building where some children were standing. She was halfway there when one of the drones spotted them. The drones immediately started to run towards them. Marie knew that she wasn't going to be able to outrun the drones with Sue barely able to walk. In desperation, she dragged Sue towards the dark forest. The drones stopped in their tracks when they saw the direction which Marie and Sue were going. The drones figured that there was no rush now. No one in their right mind would enter the dark forest. And since Marie and Sue had no other direction to go, they were as good as caught.

Marie and Sue were now at the edge of the dark forest. Marie tried to think of something to do, some way to escape the drones.

Anything would be better than going into the forest, she thought. She turned to face the drones that were slowly encircling them. Nasty came toward them, and as he approached he raised his whip above his head ready to strike them. Marie was desperate. She had no choice. She half dragged and half carried Sue into the dark forest where she knew no one would dare follow.

Chapter 10

The drones came to the edge of the dark forest. They scurried about, peering into the forest but not daring to enter. They stood there for a while wondering what to do. At last they decided to leave. One of them yelled toward the area where Marie and Sue had entered. He shouted that they would never survive the day. They snickered, shrugged their shoulders and walked back towards their quarters.

Marie dragged Sue, who could barely walk, further into the forest. When she was sure no one was following them, she laid Sue down on a soft patch of leaves and looked around. They were no more than twenty feet into the forest, but it seemed like it was twenty miles. It was very dark and foreboding looking. Marie was very worried and scared, but knew she would have to be brave, at least in front of Sue, or Sue might panic. Marie decided that the best thing they could do was try to hide themselves from any creatures that may be in the area.

Marie started to gather leaves and twigs and made a big pile where Sue was lying. As she was gathering the leaves she noticed fruits and some plants which appeared to be edible. Her father, who was a woodsman, had taught her the difference between edible and poisonous fruits and plants when she was a little girl when they used to go camping in the woods. The thought of her father made her sad. She wondered if she would ever see him again. She immediately made herself busy so as not to think about him. She fed Sue some of the fruit she had picked, and only after she had had her fill did Marie eat.

After Marie finished eating, she covered Sue with leaves and began to search the floor of the forest. She picked up several sharp stones. She then started to sharpen the end of a long stick to fashion some sort of spear out of it. They stayed where they were the rest of the day and passed the time talking about their homes. They thought about how they were going to find their way back home even if it meant going through the entire dark forest. That afternoon Marie again started working on making a spear using the sharp stone, but she became too tired to continue. She covered Sue with some more leaves and then put some on herself until they were completely covered with the leaves and twigs. She had made the area look as normal as the other ground around them. As tired as she was, she could not block out the sounds of the various wild beasts that were roaming the dark forest in search for food. She hugged Sue and kept her close to her until sleep finally came.

Chapter 11

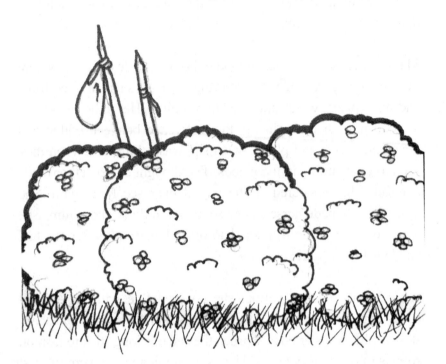

Christian felt a chill from the cool, night air. He was tired and didn't feel like moving. He finally forced himself to sit up and pick up a log to throw on the fire. As he was tossing the log on the fire, he heard something stir in the forest near him. For a second, he thought maybe he was just hearing things, after all, he was still half asleep. But no, something was nearby. He could sense it. As he dropped the log on the dwindling fire, it caused sparks to fly. At the same time, with his other hand, he reached for his sword which was lying by his side. The beast, who had been waiting for the fire to die out, realized that this was his opportunity to strike before the fire flared up again. He leapt at Christian from the forest, but was distracted for a split second by the sparks which flew when

44

Christian threw the log on the fire. This distraction gave Christian just enough time to roll to his side and avoid the slashing swing of the monsters claw which contained four inch long fingernails. Each one was as sharp and deadly as a knife. The commotion bought Winger to his feet, and he immediately became airborne and hovered over the monster. This caused the monster to look up at Winger, surprised at his sudden flight. Christian was then able to continue his roll and jump to his feet with sword at the ready. The monster tried to simultaneously strike at Winger, who was above him with one claw and Christian with the other claw, causing him to lose his balance. Christian sidestepped the blow and took advantage of the opportunity and swung his sword in an arc catching the monster in his left shoulder. The monster let out a deafening roar, and to Christian's and Winger's surprise, turned and ran back into the forest. Christian immediately took up the pursuit, but it was soon obvious to him that it was too dark and almost impossible to see. He knew that he would be in further trouble if he continued the pursuit. He decided to return to the campsite. Winger, who had been right behind him, led the way.

When Christian and Winger returned to the campsite, they started to gather the firewood, which had been strewn all over due to the struggle. They started to talk about what had just happened and the fight with the strange-looking monster. Christian described it as looking like an alligator that stood straight up and slashed with its claws. Winger agreed.

"The problem I have is what happened when you got it with your sword," Winger said.

"What do you mean?" Christian asked.

"It didn't bleed!" Winger said with a funny look on his face.

"You know, you're right," Christian responded. "I wonder why?"

"I guess it just doesn't have blood," Winger said pensively.

Just then, the monster let out another bloodcurdling roar from the forest near them, sending Christian and Winger scrambling for their shields and weapons. The roar was answered by another roar to Christian's rear. Then another.... followed by a fourth roar.

"They're all around us," Christian yelled at Winger.

"Quick, build up the fire, and let's mount up," Christian ordered.

They hurriedly threw wood on the fire, and Winger fanned it as hard as he could to get the flames going. In the meantime, Christian mounted his horse and slowly made a circle of the campsite, straining his eyes in an attempt to see into the forest.

As soon as Winger was satisfied with the fire, he grabbed his shield and spear and mounted his horse. They decided to stay near the center of the campsite, back to back in order to fend off an attack which could be coming from any direction.

"They're over there," Winger pointed into the woods to his right with his spear.

"Where… I can't see anything?" Christian responded, realizing that Winger was using his night owl vision.

"I think I can get one with my spear," Winger said.
"Go for it," Christian responded.

Winger backed his horse to the edge of the clearing, and then charging the horse forward a few steps, he leaned back and then forward and let the spear fly. His throw was fast and true. One of the monsters let out a groan and fell over. The other monsters stepped back, not realizing or understanding what was happening. They made a circle around the dead monster that was lying on the ground, motionless. They stared at him through their bloodred eyes, pondering the situation.

"I got him," Winger said with a little satisfaction and pride in his voice.

"Good shot, Winger," Christian said. "What are they doing now?" Christine continued in a curious voice.

"Nothing, they're just looking down at their dead companion," Winger responded. "I think I hit the one you wounded; it's hard to tell at this distance."

"Great, maybe they got the message and will leave us alone," Christian said hopefully.

Just then, the monsters stopped looking at the fallen beast. They slowly turned and looked toward the campsite where Winger and Christian were. Then they started to grunt and snarl.

"They seem to be working themselves into a frenzy," Winger told

Christian.

"We better get ready; anything can happen," Christian responded, grateful that Winger could see in the dark.

Then it happened. They came charging full speed at the campsite, snarling and swinging wildly with razor sharp claws.

Chapter 12

Sue woke up first. Her movement woke up Marie who was sleeping very close to her. Marie slowly moved the leaves away from her face and looked around. All seemed to be quiet except for the noises of the different forest animals and birds. She cautiously sat up and then helped Sue sit up. Sue looked much better. It probably was the fruit she fed her yesterday.

"Where are we?" Sue asked, looking around.

"We're still in the dark forest," Marie answered.

"Yes, I remember now. It all seems like a bad dream," Sue responded.

"What are we going to do, Marie?"

"Let's take it a little at a time. We can't go back to the camp. We must make it in here somehow until we can find our way home," Marie spoke pensively. She didn't want to scare Sue, but she had no idea how they were going to survive. Sue looked at her, a shiver taking control of her body.

"Well," Marie started, "let's get something to eat. There are plenty of good things growing around here." She was going to continue, but the roar of an animal stopped her mid-sentence. She looked at Sue, and they both laid back down and covered themselves with leaves again. They waited for about ten minutes, but it seemed like an eternity. They listened intently. When they didn't hear anything, they uncovered themselves and cautiously got up again and looked around. They didn't see anything, so they relaxed a bit.

"I wonder what that was," Sue said.

"I don't know, but whatever it was, I don't want anything to do with it," Marie responded.

When she was fairly certain that all was clear, Marie gathered more fruit and found some vegetables growing nearby. They ate heartily. It had been a while since they'd had fresh vegetables. They obviously grew abundantly in the forest. They were never

50

fed to the children by the drones, probably because no one would enter the forest to get them.

After they finished eating, Marie started working on her spear again. Sue watched her, fascinated by Marie's rapidly moving hands. With one hand she held the sharp stone and moved it back and forth at the end of the stick which she rotated with the other hand. It was slow and tedious. The stone didn't remove much wood with each pass. After a while, Marie paused and picked up a different stone and started again.

Sue felt much better. She told Marie that she was going to go back toward the village to see what, if anything, was going on. Marie didn't like the idea of being separated, but Sue convinced her that she would only be several feet away. She promised not to lose sight of where Marie was.

Sue made her way to the edge of the dark forest and peaked into the village containing the hovels that had been her home. No one seemed to be around. *They are probably all out on the work detail,* she thought. She looked toward where the kitchen was and wondered if she could sneak into it and obtain some food. Her thoughts were quickly interrupted when she saw one of the children come out of the kitchen carrying a bucket. He slowly walked toward the area where the garbage pails were and emptied the bucket into one of the pails. Sue was about to call out to him when a drone came out and stood by the kitchen door watching the actions of the boy. The boy then slowly walked back into the kitchen followed by the drone. Sue decided that there was nothing she could do. It was time to return to where Marie was. She didn't want Marie to worry about her.

After Sue returned, they decided that they would walk deeper into the forest to see if they could find a path that would lead them somewhere. It didn't take long before they found a small path that appeared to have been made by the animals wandering the forest. The path made it much easier to walk, and they both allowed themselves to dream that perhaps this path would lead them to the other side of the forest and home. Marie was in the lead, her newly made spear in hand and at the ready.

They walked for about forty uneventful minutes and were beginning to feel less apprehensive about their plight. Then it happened! The path just seemed to give way under their feet and they fell into a deep hole that had been covered over to look like the rest of the path. When Marie landed, she fell on the middle of her spear which quickly snapped in two. *Lucky,* she thought, *I didn't fall on the sharp end.* They got up and looked around. They were trapped in a hole with no way to get out.

"What are we going to do?" Sue asked.

"I don't know," Marie answered, looking around at the walls of the hole which were holding them prisoner. She didn't say anything to Sue, but she realized that they were probably caught by some monster or animal that was using the trap to catch its dinner.

Chapter 13

Christian and Winger braced themselves for battle. They had their swords drawn and their shields protecting one side of their bodies. Even the horses sensed they were about to get into a fight, as they nervously pranced in place, their nostrils flaring. Then it happened, the beasts came charging blindly out of the woods towards the two combatants who were prepared and waiting for them. They came at them three abreast. Winger's spear had finished the fourth one who was lying dead in the woods, the spear impaled in its chest. One beast ran directly at Christian, swinging at him with its dagger-like claws. Its first blow struck the horse's breastplate and glanced off. Before it had a chance to swing again, Christian maneuvered his horse to get a clear shot at the beast. He leaned forward and down and thrust his sword with all his might at the beast. His sword found its mark and entered the beast's chest. This time there was no roar, the beast gasped and fell backwards, dead. Christian immediately pulled back and retrieved his sword. He then looked over at Winger who was holding two beasts at bay. Winger was defending himself well. One beast had attacked on his left, swinging wildly at him. Winger deflected the blows with his shield as he swung his sword at the one on the right, keeping it at a distance. Christian immediately moved his horse to Winger's left and with one blow, dispatched the beast that Winger was fending off using his shield. Winger was then free to pursue the other beast and ran it through with his sword, ending the battle as quickly as it had begun.

They dismounted and surveyed the battle scene. Christian studied the bodies of the three beasts in the campsite, while Winger entered the woods to retrieve his spear. When he returned, they sat and discussed the battle. Then they decided to have a close look at their adversaries. They examined the beasts, looking at them very closely, trying to discover what they were. The answer came when they rolled one beast over. It had small growths on its back which would one day become wings.

"Could it be?" Winger asked, not believing what he was thinking.

"I think so," Christian responded.

"Why didn't they breathe fire?" Winger continued?

"I think that they were just too young," was Christian's answer.

"Do you think these are the dragon's offspring?" Winger mused.

"I think so," Christian answered. "But what worries me is the thought that there may be more out there," he said, motioning towards the forest that surrounded them.

"Just think about it," Winger said. "These four could have grown to be fully-fledged dragons. I wonder what would have happened had they survived."

"Had they grown to full size, there probably would be no stopping them. They would probably take over the world," Christian answered. "Then, if there are others, they must be stopped now before it's too late. I wonder how many offspring a dragon has," Winger asked.

"I don't know," Christian answered, "but I hope this is all of them."

It didn't take long for their questions to be answered. A roar emanating from the dark forest behind them gave them the answer they dreaded. Again, that roar was answered by another roar and then another. Christian and Winger looked at each other in disbelief.

"What should we do now?" Winger asked.

"I think we should get out of here before we're surrounded by them," Christian responded.

They mounted their horses and started down the trail further into the dark forest. They deliberately held themselves back from galloping at a high rate of speed, even though they wanted to. They feared that the horses might get hurt running through the heavily-foliaged forest. They didn't get very far. The trail was blocked! Someone had deliberately placed trees and brush across it.

The trail had funneled them into a path that was very narrow, so they couldn't turn their horses around. They dismounted and looked around to try and find a way out. They could barely walk past the horses due to the narrowness of the path. The horses started to get nervous realizing they were trapped by the path with nowhere to go. Just then, the roars started again, this time behind them and getting closer fast.

Chapter 14

Marie began digging at the wall of the hole with the sharp end of the broken spear.

"Take the other part of the spear, and try to scrap out holes that we can use for steps," she said to Sue.

Sue complied, but the end of the spear she had was not sharp, the dirt was very hard, and she could barely make a mark in it as she scraped with all her might.

They had worked at it for about ten minutes when they heard something approaching the hole that had become their prison. They stopped their work and huddled in a corner of the hole, staring up at the opening. They could hear heavy breathing coming from above. After a few minutes of listening to the heavy breathing, the head of a huge lion appeared in the opening, looking down at them.

"What shall we do?" Sue asked Marie in a terror-stricken voice.

"I don't know, but if he jumps down here, we're goners," Marie answered.

The lion looked at them but didn't move. It stayed at the opening just looking at the two small figures huddled together in a corner of the hole.

"He must have just eaten," Marie observed, "or he'd have jumped down here already".

"Maybe he's saving us for later," Sue responded with fear in each word.

Just then, the lion laid down with its two front paws hanging over the edge of the hole and made himself comfortable by resting his head on the paws as if prepared to take a nap.

"What should we do?" Sue asked. "He looks like he's there to stay or until he gets hungry".

"We can't just sit here and do nothing," Marie observed.

Marie slowly got up and moved toward the end of the hole where the lion was resting. She waved her broken spear at the lion and yelled, "Shoo, shoo". The lion lazily raised its head and looked at her as if to say, "Don't bother me". Marie, lead on by the lion not making any sudden moves, became more and more brazen. She yelled at the lion in a loud voice and finally jumped up and struck the lion's paw with the end of the spear. The lion looked at her and growled. Marie was determined. Figuring she had nothing to lose anyway, continued her poking and shouting. The lion finally stood up out of the reach of the broken spear, but Marie continued her tirade. The lion playfully pawed at the spear as Marie jumped up, jabbing at him. Finally, bored with the little game, the lion moved away.

"Do you think he left?" Sue asked.

"I don't know, but we can't stay here. Let's keep digging," Marie responded.

They went back to work but had little success. It was starting to get dark already when they barely finished two steps. Marie calculated that it would take at least three more steps before they could climb out and now the only way they could dig would be for one of them to climb on the other in order to dig at a higher level in the hole. This would take much longer and be more difficult.

They were about to give up for the night, when they heard an awful roar. It wasn't a lion, but a terrible eerie roar that shook the two of them causing a shiver to run up and down their spines. Once again they huddled in the corner of the hole, and once again they were looked down upon from above. Only this time the beast that looked down on them had a head that looked like an alligator and was peering at them through blood red eyes.

Chapter 15

Christian looked at Winger and then to the horses that were trapped in the wedge formed by the trees. The roars and grunts of the beasts could be clearly heard now and getting closer by the second.

"I'll run down the path towards them and try to hold them off," Christian said. "You try to back the horses out and get them free."

"I don't know about that," Winger answered with a tone of worry in his voice. "There may be a whole bunch of them."

"The narrow path works in my favor too," Christian responded. "I'll try to find a spot where they can only get through one at a time and make my stand; in the meantime get the horses free, and then join me."

"Good luck, I'll see you in a few minutes," Winger answered trying to sound upbeat.

Christian headed back down the path that they had just come from. He got about twenty yards or so away from where Winger and the horses were, when he spotted a good area for their defense. The path was narrow at that point, and it had a little rise to it on Christian's side which would give him additional height and advantage. The roars and grunts were getting much louder now as Christian took his position, shield and sword ready. There was not much else he could do except to wait for them.

Winger went to the front of the horse and spoke softly to it in reassuring tones. The horse was frightened, and the sounds of the grunts and roars did not help the situation. He patted the horse and slowly pushed against it to try to get it to back out. The horse didn't budge. Try as hard as he could, the horse just wouldn't move. Winger decided that it was the sounds coming from the rear in the direction of where the beasts were coming, that were causing the horse not to back up and free itself. Winger was getting desperate. He wanted to free the horses quickly so that he could join his partner and help him in the fight with the beasts, but the horse wasn't moving. He decided he would have to drown out the sounds of the beasts if he was going to make any headway. He took a deep breath and starting to sing as loudly as he could. He felt foolish, singing to the horse in such a loud voice, but it was working; the horse was calming down. Soon the horse responded to his pushing and backed out of the trap. He finally got it past the edge of the trap and turned it around and tied its reins to some bushes. He then went back and continuing to sing as loud as he could, backed the other horse out and also tied it nearby. Finished with his task, Winger immediately started running back down the path in the direction that Christian had gone.

Christian didn't have to wait too long before the beasts were in sight. He counted at least six of them coming down the trail grunting and roaring as if to bolster their courage ....or.... perhaps to scare opponents. One of them seemed a little bigger than the others. Christian wondered if perhaps he was the leader. They spotted Christian waiting for them. They stopped dead in their tracks as if they were assessing the situation. By their actions, Christian came to the conclusion that they weren't very smart or perhaps just extremely slow. At least by a human's standard. After a minute or so of grunting to each other, one of them charged at Christian. He was waiting for it. He extended his sword and pointed it directly at the beast who practically ran into it. It was only at the last minute that it realized what it was doing and stopped and began to flail its arms but it was too late. All Christian had to do was lunge forward a little. He struck the beast a fatal blow with the point of his sword. He immediately extracted the sword and looked at the other beasts to figure out what they were going to do. Two of them started to go off on each side of the path in an obvious attempt to try and get around Christian and probably try to attack him from the rear while another beast came directly at him. Christian noticed that the bigger one stayed back. The beast that came straight at Christian began flailing its arms but staying at a distance far enough so as to avoid his sword. *Perhaps I underestimated them,* Christian thought. He's trying to get me to move out of the higher and narrow part of the path, and he's also keeping me busy while his cohorts try to get around me through the thick brush. Christian lunged at the beast in front of him, but the beast just backed up in an attempt to get Christian to follow him out of the narrow part of the path. When their ploy didn't work, the beast backed off, and the bigger one approached Christian. He stayed about ten feet away and just stood there grunting at Christian. Christian could hear the beasts on his right and left starting to make headway in their attempt to get around him. *That was probably what this big one was waiting for,* he thought. Christian decided to take action. He charged at the beast who backpedaled, avoiding the sword. It was a mistake. Two other beasts charged at Christian side by side. Christian swung his sword from side to side catching one beast at his shoulder and forcing the other to step aside to avoid a blow. Christian started to step backwards to get back into the narrow part of the path when the beast that was not hit started to charge again. He lunged at Christian who met him head on with his sword piercing the beast's stomach. The beast was seriously wounded, however, its forward motion knocked Christian backwards, and he fell on the ground. In his attempt to keep his balance, Christian had to let go of his sword which was still in the beast. The large beast, seeing Christian's fall to the ground, immediately attacked. He jumped on top of Christian, straddling him. He raised his claw with its razor sharp nails and slammed it down towards Christian's face. Christian managed to move slightly under the weight of the beast, but the blow caught him on the side of his head, cutting his scalp and making him feel dizzy. The beast raised him claw again, this time to finish off Christian.

Chapter 16

Marie held Sue tightly as they huddled in the corner of the hole. The monster wasn't looking in the hole anymore, but they could hear it walking around above them. This continued for about fifteen minutes when a strange thing happened. A growl came from somewhere else up above the hole. They figured it was the lion coming back, and maybe he didn't like the monster being at the hole which was holding the two girls captive.

The monster let out a roar, but this time it was a little further away from the hole. Then the lion growled again and it began! Growls and yelps and roars and the shaking of trees and branches could be clearly heard coming from above their underground prison.

"They must be fighting," Marie concluded, half talking to Sue and half thinking out loud.

"What shall we do?" asked Sue, her voice quivering.

"There's nothing we can do, we're trapped down here," Marie answered.

They looked at each other and decided they would try digging the steps again. At least it gave them something to do and made them feel as though they had some control over their lives.

The fighting seemed to be going on forever and getting more ferocious. Growls and roars and the scuffling of leaves and branches could be clearly heard.

And then it happened. The girls were just starting to dig at the side of the hole when a thick vine came over the edge and into the hole. The girls looked up, and there was the head of a boy looking down at them with his finger across his lips motioning them to be quiet and not to speak. He then signaled them to grab the vine and climb up. Marie handed the vine to Sue. She then pushed Sue up the vine first, worrying that she may still be a little weak and have difficulty climbing out of the hole. As Sue got to the top of the hole the boy helped her out and motioned for her to go along a small path. Sue refused. She wanted to wait for Marie. Meanwhile, the fight between the monster and the lion continued and sounded like it was getting worse. Sue could see the bushes moving where the sounds were coming from and realized that at any moment they could be spotted by the fighting beasts. The fight was taking place only about twenty feet from them. Finally, Marie's head came to the surface, and the boy and Sue helped her over the edge of the hole. Once again the boy motioned to be quiet and to go up the path, only this time he lead them, running as fast as he could with the girls trying to keep up.

They had no sooner started running when Marie noticed that the fight had stopped, and except for their own heavy breathing, it got very quiet. Marie was pushing Sue, who was in front of her, and trying to get her to run faster. She then passed Sue and held her by the wrist pulling her along in an attempt to help her run faster. They finally came to a cave, and the boy ran into it, followed by Sue and Marie. When they entered the cave they saw other boys and girls who were inside, but they had no time to talk. They were all pointing toward the path where Marie and Sue had just come from. They had fear written all over their faces.

Marie looked out of the cave towards the path which had just lead them to the cave, and her heart sunk. Coming down the path towards them, half walking and half running, was the monster. It was huge and had big red eyes. It looked like an overgrown alligator that could walk upright. They were trapped in the cave, and the beast seemed to know it as it looked at them and just kept coming.

Chapter 17

Christian tried to grab the beast's arm so that it would not strike him again but couldn't do it. He was too dizzy from the first blow. He figured that he was finished. The only thing that could save him would be a miracle.

After the frustrating time he had trying to move the horses, Winger was finally approaching the area of the battle where Christian was fighting with the beasts. He had run as fast as he could and was ready to do battle again with those weird beasts, dragons or whatever they were. He was not, however, prepared for the sight that greeted him as he approached the narrow part of the path where Christian was supposed to hold off the beasts until his arrival. There was Christian lying on the ground, bleeding from the head, and being straddled by one of the beasts. His hand raised, and he was about to strike Christian again. Winger, without thinking, immediately threw his spear with all the strength he could muster toward the beast. The beast took the brunt of the spear in his right shoulder. It caused him to fall sideways.

Christian couldn't believe it. His miracle had arrived in the form of a spear. As the beast fell sideways, its weight shifted from on top of Christian, allowing him to wiggle out from under him. Christian immediately took out his dagger from its scabbard on his belt and plunged it into the beast before it could recover from its fall. The beast, not believing that it's victory over Christian was turned into defeat, tried in vain to regain its balance but could not. It closed its eyes, let out a final grunt and died.

"Watch out!" Christian yelled at Winger. "There are a couple of them in the woods, trying to get around us."

Christian moved forward to retrieve his weapons, when he realized that one of the beasts was still standing there on the path. The beast looked at Christian, grunted and slowly walked down the path in the opposite direction away from Christian and Winger.

"I guess he's had enough," Winger said while peering into the woods where he thought he heard a twig snap.

"We can't let them get way," Christian said while wiping away some blood that had trickled down from his forehead and into one of his eyes.

"Don't forget, it will grow into a dragon someday and probably terrorize half the countryside."

But it was too late; the beast had disappeared in the thick foliage.

"Look out!" Christian yelled at Winger, as a beast exited the woods behind Winger.

Winger spun around and dispatched the beast with a wide swing of his sword. At almost the same time, the other beast exited from the other side of the woods. Winger pivoted quickly. He didn't have time to think but had to rely on his instincts. Just as quickly as the first, the second beast met the same fate at the hands of Winger and his trusty swift sword.

"That was close," Christian said to Winger.
"You're telling me," Winger responded.

"How did that big one get the better of you anyway?" Winger asked.

"I don't have time to explain now; let's get the horses and see if we can catch up to the one that got away."

"By the way," Christian said, "what was all that singing about? I was fighting for my life and you're enjoying yourself singing in the woods. I don't really mind. But to make matters worse, you can't even carry a tune." Christian half chuckled, trying to release the tension of the previous terror.

"Have you ever heard an owl say anything but 'hoot' before?" Winger responded.

"The horses were spooked by the growls of the beasts, and the only way I could get them to move was to drown out their growls with my melodious tunes." Winger was in a giddy mood brought on by the strain of the battle.

They reached the horses and mounted up. They galloped back down the path in pursuit of the beast that had gotten away.

Christian fashioned a bandage for his head from a piece of cloth as they swiftly galloped down the path in the direction they had originally come from in rapid pursuit of the beast.

It didn't take long to catch up to it at the rate of speed they were traveling. The beast turned to face them and swung wildly with its razor sharp claws at Christian. The blows glanced off the armor on the horse as it reared up at the sight of the beast. This made Christian too high for the beast to reach. Christian countered the attack and plunged his sword into his red-eyed enemy who fell back onto the ground, mortally wounded.

As Christian was replacing his sword in its scabbard, he heard the roar of the dragon again. He looked back at Winger who was right behind him. They decided to follow the sounds.

It didn't take long before they came upon a clearing in the woods. They dismounted and tied their horses to a tree and cautiously crawled toward the clearing.

What they saw caused Christian to shiver. It was the dragon, and it was much bigger than it had looked when it flew over them. Around the dragon were several of the red- eyed beasts. They had been right; these beasts were the offspring of the dreaded dragon.

71

Now what???

How were they ever going to defeat such a huge creature??? Who knows how many of the offspring there are running about in the woods???

They knew that the dragon and its beast offspring will make their quest to save the children almost impossible.

Chapter 18

Marie and Sue, after running as hard as they could to get into the cave, couldn't believe that the beast was going to get them after all they had been through. It was getting closer and closer. Then the boy that had rescued them shouted, "Let it go". With that, Marie noticed that a few of the other children, some on each side of the cave opening, were holding a long rope-like vine. At the boy's shout, they let go of the vines and a huge log with spikes of wood came crashing down from above the opening to the cave. The spikes were smaller branches which were sharpened and acted like spears, sticking out in all directions. It completely covered the opening to the cave, making it impossible for anything larger than a medium- sized dog to enter.

The beast stopped in its tracks, surprised by this turn of events. Marie and Sue could see it clearly. There was only about ten feet between themselves and the beast. Gratefully the log was lying between them. Nevertheless, they were still frightened by its grotesque looks and searing red eyes. It was obvious that the beast had been injured in the struggle with the lion. It had scratch marks on its chest and shoulders.

The beast snarled and looked around the log in an attempt to see if there was any way to bypass it and get into the cave, but it couldn't find any. It walked back and forth from one end of the log to the other. It did this several times, and then it snarled again, swung a clawed hand half heartily at some of the spikes and finally walked away in frustration.

Marie and Sue were so happy to see the beast leave, they hugged each other. As the excitement subsided, Marie looked around the cave. What she saw was hard to believe. There were about fifteen children in the cave, some of whom she recognized as children the drones had taken away from the compound for being unproductive. She then looked at the boy who had saved them from the hole and certain death.

He smiled at her and said, "I bet you're surprised to see us, aren't you?"

"I sure am," Marie said awkwardly. "How did you all get here?"

"First," he said, "let me introduce you to everyone. My name is Tom," he started, and then he introduced everyone in the cave, one by one.

Marie responded, "I'm Marie, and this is Sue, and we are sure happy to see all of you".

Tom told their stories as some of the children started a fire and busily began cooking and making preparations to eat.

"You see, we were all either thrown into the dark forest by the drones as unproductive, or some of us, including myself, escaped into the dark forest on our own. I don't know about you two, but I was sick of starving and being pushed around by Mustgreed and his drones and figured anything was better than that. I took my chances one night and made a run for it. I thought I was a goner a couple of times, but then lo and behold, I found two others who had been forced into the forest by the drones. We found this cave and made it our business to check for others every opportunity we had. Eventually all fifteen of us, or should I say, seventeen of us now, came together. It really wasn't bad. There has been plenty of food and fresh water in the river back there," he pointed over his shoulder, "and until the beasts started showing up a few weeks ago, it was relatively quiet. Most of the animals we were able to scare off because there were many of us, but the beasts weren't afraid at all. I think they're fearless, but thank goodness, very dumb. At any rate, we found this cave and built the defense log. As you can see, it works pretty well. It's kept us pretty safe till now. The only problem with the log is that it is so heavy that we have a difficult time rolling it back up. It takes all the strength all of us have".

Marie didn't know what to say. She was still stunned at seeing all the children and happy at the thought that she and Sue would no longer be alone. There is safety in numbers…

Chapter 19

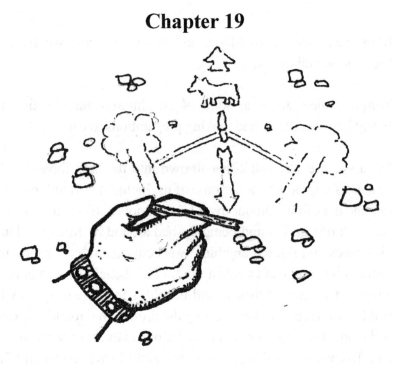

Christian and Winger backed away from the clearing, and after putting a considerable distance between themselves and the clearing, set up camp for the night. They tried to sleep, and although both of them were exhausted from the battles of the day, they found it difficult due to the thought of the dragon and the beasts.

"Somehow we're going to have to kill that dragon and the beasts if we're ever going to make it through the dark forest," Christian said.

"Easier said than done," Winger responded. "Did you see the size of it?"

"Yes, we have to think of something ingenious....but what?" Christian pondered.

"You're the wise old owl," he kidded Winger, "Think of something."

"We'll never be able to attack it head on," Winger said half thinking out loud. "We're going to have to trick it or trap it somehow, but how do you trap something that's the size of a house?"

They spent a restless night. They didn't dare light a fire because they were so close to danger.

The sun was high in the sky by the time they woke up. Exhausted by the events of the day before, they had slept longer than they wanted to. It was dangerous not to be alert in the dark forest.

They struggled to their feet and began to get their thoughts together. Pictures of dragons and beasts with red eyes were never far from their thoughts.

They ate a quick breakfast and were preparing to move out, when suddenly they realized they had nowhere to go until they defeated the dragon. They looked at each other and sat back down on the ground deep in thought.

"It's too big to trap in any sort of hole," Christian said, knowing he didn't have to explain to Winger what he was talking about.

"I know. I was thinking that we would have to kill it by

err...perhaps attacking it from the rear," Winger responded.

"How do we do that?" Christian questioned. "Our weapons would have no effect on it at all."

"That's it, we have to get bigger and better weapons," Winger said.

"I agree, but we're in the dark forest, and I haven't seen any weapons stores in here," Christian said factiously.

"No, but maybe we could make some," Winger answered. "I remember watching some workers making catapults for the knights before they went off to storm a castle."

"That's a good idea," Christian responded, "but we haven't the tools, the time, or the knowledge to build one".

Winger pondered Christian's answer. "I bet if we tried we could come up with something. Let's see, a catapult would be ideal. We could load a big rock on it and pull it back and let it go right at the dragon's head."

"How do we pull it back or for that matter move a stone big enough to do the job? There is only you and I," Christian questioned.

"I guess you're right," Winger sounded dejected. "Wait a minute," he continued. "If we could find two hickory trees close together near the edge of the clearing that the dragon is in, maybe we could....make a slingshot of some sort," he thought out loud. "Yes, that might work."

Christian's eyes lit up. "I think you may have something," he answered. "But say we get lucky and find the trees, what do we use to shoot at the dragon, and how do we propel it?"

Winger was getting excited as the ideas buzzed around in his head. "We can braid vines together; lord knows there are plenty of them in the forest. We can use that to tie between the trees and make it a large bow out of the 2 trees. Then we can cut some small trees and sharpen the ends of them and make them into giant arrows."

"Great," Christian responded. Then his face started to drop as he thought, "How do we pull the strings err...vines back far enough to propel the shafts or arrows or whatever? We're not that strong. Even the two of us together couldn't do it with enough force to travel a distance and spear the dragon".

Winger's shoulders visibly sagged as he realized that Christian was right. The whole plan seemed so plausible until now. "Let me think about that one for a while," he said.

Winger walked over to where the horses were and started to pet them as he mulled the problem over and over in his mind. Then he leapt up into the air, scaring the horses and causing them to jump. He had a big grin on his face that made Christian sure he had come up with an idea.

"We can use the horses," he said triumphantly. "We can tie the vines onto their saddle with an addition cord between the vines and the saddle. Then we walk them back until the vines are taut and the trees bend and then cut the added on cord and let it fly. Just think of the power it will have."

Christian pondered the idea. Winger cleared some leaves and debris from the ground and drew a rough picture with a pointed stick.

"It just might work," Christian said, a smile covering his face.

Chapter 20

After dinner, Sue and Marie chatted with their new friends in the cave. They had difficulty containing themselves because they were so happy and excited. They talked and talked and talked to anyone who would listen. Most of the children understood and were also glad to have them as new-found friends.

Sue seemed to have been cured. She was no longer listless or weak. She seemed to thrive being around the other children, mainly because they were not depressed. The children in the camp were always depressed due to the hard work, little food and being the captives of Mustgreed. She realized how happy she was just to be free, even though she knew she was still lost and in the dark forest. Things did seem so much better because of the other children.

Before they knew it, it was time to go to bed. Some of the children shared their assortment of leaves and dried grass that they used for a ground cover. Sue and Marie made themselves mattresses and nestled in for the night. They were glad to see that the spiked log covering the front of the cave entrance was kept in place during the night.

Sue looked over at Marie as she lay on her makeshift bed, and they smiled at each other, knowing inside how happy they were even if it might be short lived.

For the first night in a long time, they rested comfortably.

Chapter 21

Christian and Winger decided to leave the horses in the campsite and head out to the edge of the large clearing where the dragon made its home.

When they arrived near the clearing they were surprised at how close they had camped to it. They both got down on all fours and crawled to the edge. The dragon was there, about three-hundred yards away at the opposite end of the clearing. It was just lying there with its head resting on the ground.

"It may be sleeping," Christian said.

"I hope so," Winger responded.

"Let's crawl along the edge of the clearing and get a little closer," Christian said. "We would never be able to get an effective shot at it from this distance."

Winger agreed, and they began to crawl along the edge of the clearing, using the bushes and trees for cover. They crawled closer and closer to the huge dragon.

When they felt they were close enough, they studied the clearing nearby looking for the ideal trees with which to fashion their huge bow and arrow. Christian motioned to Winger and pointed to a spot along the edge of the clearing that appeared to contain two trees that seemed to fit the bill.

"Let's move back from the clearing so we can talk," Christian whispered.

Winger nodded his approval, and they slowly crawled backwards away from the clearing and further into the dark forest.

When they were far enough from the dragon, they sat down and began to make their plans.

"Those trees I pointed out look like they could do it," Christian said.

"I don't know about that," Winger responded, "they're too close to the edge of the clearing. We'll never be able to work on them without the dragon seeing us".

"But we can't go much further into the forest, we'll never be able to shoot through the trees," Christian answered.

They sat there for a while as they pondered their dilemma.

"Let's take another look at it. Maybe we can figure something out," Christian suggested.

They once again crawled to the clearing, only this time they made their way to where the trees were. They motioned to each other using made-up sign language. Christian pointed to some branches, which would have to be cut off, flailing wildly with a make believe axe. After that, Winger imitated a horse straining against the vines that would be attached to the trees. By using this method, they were able to plan the work they had ahead of them. While they were doing this, they kept a wary eye on the dragon that didn't seem to move. They felt they were out of hearing distance, as long as they were reasonably quiet, but then again, who knows how sharp the hearing of a dragon is?

Winger began pacing off the distance between the trees and where he estimated the horse would start its straining power pull in order to figure the length of vines they would need. He was halfway through his task when he looked up, and standing in front of him was one of the beasts. The beast, though startled, quickly sprang at Winger. Winger, just as startled as the beast, reacted without thinking by sidestepping out of the way of the beast's flailing, dagger-like claws. The forward motion of the beast carried him past Winger and directly at Christian, who was about twenty feet behind Winger. Christian drew his sword and held it in front of him and the inertia of the beast's forward movement caused him to impale himself on it. Then it happened! The beast let out a groan as it continued forward and fell to the ground causing Christian's sword to continue through its body. Both Christian and Winger felt a cold shiver go through their bodies at the thought that the dragon may have heard the groan of its offspring. They slowing turned their attention from the beast to the clearing where the dragon was. The dragon looked up in their direction. Christian and Winger thought for sure they were goners. But then, as if to shrug, the dragon laid its head back down on the ground.

Christian and Winger decided that they had better drag the body of the dead beast away from the clearing and the area where they were going to have to work to set up their huge weapon.

The beast was heavy, but after Christian removed his sword, they managed to drag it far enough away from the area that they would be working in. They hid it under some bushes and covered it as best they could to conceal it from any other beasts that might be heading for the clearing.

Back in their camp, they thought about the chores that lay ahead of them.

Winger almost immediately started to gather long vines which appeared to be strong enough for the job. He tested them by tugging on them, and when he felt he had enough, he started to braid them into a thick strong rope.

"You don't suppose that those trees we selected are on a path that the beasts used to get to the dragon, do you?" Christian asked pensively.

"I don't know," Winger responded, having not thought of that unfortunate possibility.

"I guess we'll have to work with one eye on the forest and the other on our job. We'll have to watch the dragon at the same time," Christian responded.

"I was thinking," Winger said changing the subject, "how are we going to work that close to the dragon and practically in the open? We have to chop branches and set the whole thing up; he's bound to hear us or see us."

"We'll just wait until he leaves to do our work," Christian answered, his confidence in his plan waning.

Chapter 22

Sue and Marie woke up feeling refreshed. They had slept a long time. The children in the cave had already eaten their breakfast and were busily cleaning up. Some of the children offered them fruit, which the girls gladly accepted and ate quickly, having suddenly discovered their lost appetites and how very hungry they were.

After breakfast, Tom explained to them that all the children were assigned chores that they had to do and that Sue and Marie would have to do their share. Tom asked Sue to go with some of the children to get water from the stream that was located on the other side of the hill where the cave was located. Marie was assigned the task of assisting with the cleanup of the cave. She didn't like being separated from Sue but felt that she would be alright as long as there were other children around.

Sue and the other children left the cave that afternoon to get the water. Before they could leave the log was lifted from the entrance. Tom had explained that they normally lift the log only high enough to crawl under, in hopes of discouraging any animals or beasts from attempting to enter. It was so heavy that it had taken almost all the children tugging at the thick vines to lift the log.

They walked along a narrow path carrying large gourds that were hollowed out with vines for handles. The gourds would serve as canteens in which they would transport the water. The vines made the gourds a little easier to carry since they could sling it over their shoulder. One of the boys had two large gourds, one on each end of a pole, which he carried across his shoulders.
There were five of them including Sue. The water party was led by a young girl whose name was Peggy and who obviously knew her way. She skirted bushes and walked around trees with ease. Before they left the cave, Peggy had warned Sue not to break any branches or leave any traces of them that an animal might be able to follow. As they slowly made their way, every so often Peggy would stop and signal everyone to crouch down. She was very cautious, but Sue didn't want it any other way.

Finally, Sue could hear the gurgling of a running stream. As they approached, Peggy again signaled everyone to stop. At this time Sue was near the lead because Peggy wanted her close by since this was Sue's first trip. Peggy looked at Sue and pointed to the stream. Sue could see a baby deer drinking from the stream and felt a tug at her heart. It reminded her of how she and her father would watch the deer for hours when they went out into the woods. Sue didn't have much time for daydreaming. Peggy had explained that this was the most dangerous part of the trip because they could never tell when a beast or lion might come to the stream for water.

They quickly filled their gourds and started back towards the cave. Sue was having some difficulty carrying the gourd because it would swing as she walked and bump into her side causing some of the water to spill out and get her wet. She finally discovered that if she slung the vine behind her neck and held the gourd with both hands in front of her she would not spill as much.

They climbed a hill which took them above and to the rear of the cave. Peggy explained that she would like to go back in this direction as it gave her a good view of the area in front of the cave. Once again, Peggy signaled for them to be quiet and to crouch down. Sue struggled with the gourd and took it off her neck as it almost tipped over when she knelt down. This distraction lasted for only a second and was quickly dispelled by the roar of the beast who was below them,trying once again to get past the log with the spikes in order to get in the cave and at the children. Sue shuddered at the thought of Marie in the cave facing this beast. She said a silent prayer that it would go away.

Then it happened! With her complete attention being diverted to what was happening at the cave entrance, Sue unintentionally let go of her gourd. It immediately started rolling down the hill spilling the water as it went. It gathered speed careening down the hill. Sue's heart was in her throat as the gourd headed straight for the beast. It then flew over the top of the cave and landed on the log with the spikes that was guarding the entrance to the cave and burst into pieces. The beast, who was taken by surprise, looked at the shattered gourd and then turned its gaze upward in the direction it had come from. The movement over the top of the cave caught its attention. Then he spotted what appeared to be a girl. The beast quickly decided to leave the cave entrance and investigate.

Peggy realized that they were spotted and quickly told everyone to split up and run in different directions in hopes of confusing the beast. In her mind she felt that it would be better to sacrifice herself to the beast so that the other children might make it to the cave. She hesitated long enough for the beast to see her. She stared intently at it waiting long enough for it to commit itself and go after her before she would attempt to run. What she had not realized was that Sue had remained back and was just a few feet behind her. When Peggy realized that Sue was still there, she immediately grabbed her hand and started running as fast as she could. Both girls were very fast runners, but the forest was so thick that it was difficult to maneuver and make any headway. The beast didn't have this problem. Although it was much slower than the girls, it just lumbered its way through the brush in a straight line toward the girls with little or no effort.

The girls tried to quickly make headway through the forest, but the brush was so thick that the beast was gaining on them. Then Peggy spotted it. It was a path that had been made through the brush. It was their only chance to get away. They ran like the wind down the path. Peggy looked back over her shoulder and was elated to see that they were putting distance between themselves and the beast. She looked over at Sue who was running as fast as she could, and was just a little behind her, and gave her the thumbs up sign. Then something totally unexpected happened. Just when they thought they could get away, they both tripped over something that was lying on the ground. It caused them to lose their balance and fall. Because of their rapid forward motion, they tumbled over and over, scrambling on the ground. This was all the snarling beast needed to catch up to them. It straddled them and raised its razor sharp claw ready to cut the girls to ribbons.

Chapter 23

Christian and Winger woke up the next morning at daybreak. They ate some fruits and nuts and decided to continue making the various vines they needed before going back to the clearing. It was almost noon by the time they decided to throw the vines over one of the horses and lead it to the clearing.

When they felt they were close enough, they tied the reins of the horse to a nearby tree and crawled to the edge of the clearing. The dragon was almost in the same position they had seen it in the day before. They returned to where they had left the horse and gingerly took the vines off and laid them on the ground about fifty feet in the forest from the clearing. They laid the vines on a path that was already being forged from them and the horse walking back and forth between the clearing and their campsite. They decided that Winger should bring the horse back to the campsite while Christian kept an eye on the dragon to try to find out what it did all day and when it left. After Winger started back, Christian, once again, crawled to the edge of the clearing and found a spot where he could clearly see the dragon. After satisfying himself that he was hidden from the dragon, and he could not be easily be spotted, he relaxed.

The warm sun and the soft grass on which he was lying almost put Christian to sleep. It was only when the dragon rose to its feet, causing the ground to shutter, that Christian was bought back to reality. He put his hand to his forehead in an attempt to block the sun from his eyes and get a better view of the dragon. The huge monster raised its fierce-looking head upward toward the sky and with much effort began flapping its huge wings. It took several movements of its wings before it ungracefully took off.

Christian watched it as it hovered off the ground for a while and then flew off toward the sun.

It was only when Christian was certain that the dragon was far enough away that he decided it was safe to get up. He stretched and began to walk toward the trees that would eventually become a gigantic bow and arrow. He no sooner arrived where the trees were located when Winger returned.

"The dragon left," Christian volunteered.

"I thought so," Winger responded. "Let's get busy while we can."

Christian and Winger removed their swords from their scabbards and after giving a quick look towards the clearing where the dragon had been and satisfying themselves that it was gone, began to chop some of the lower branches from the trees. It only took minutes as the branches came hurling off with each swing of the sharp swords. When they finished, they stepped back to look at their handy work and decide what they were going to do next.

"We have to find a straight smaller tree to make the arrow," Winger said.

"Maybe we should make a few," Christian responded.

"I don't know if we would get a chance at another shot," Winger said, a little anxiety in his voice.
They walked into the forest eyeing the trees and looking for just the right ones.

Winger was the first to spot one using his sharp owl eyes.

"There," he said motioning to Christian to look to his right.

"Yes, that'll do perfectly," Christian smiled.

They chopped at it swinging with downward strokes with their swords so as to make a point at the same time that they cut it down. It took a while for the tree to fall as it was a hardwood tree and about five inches in diameter. When they finally felled it, they sat next to it and rested.

"I think we should chop the branches off it, and then we can get one of the horses to drag it to the other trees," Christian suggested. "Then we'll look for some more just in case we do get more than one shot."

Before they could begin, they heard the unmistakable sound of the wings of the dragon flapping against the wind and getting closer and closer. They looked at each other and then up at the sky in the direction of the noise in an effort to get a glimpse of the foreboding monster. Unfortunately, the forest was too thick. They decided to go to the clearing to see if the dragon landed in the same place. If it did, they reasoned they could set up their shot aiming in that general area.

They crawled to the clearing, and there it was. As huge as ever, the dragon sat there in the same place. While they watched, two beasts came out of the forest near the dragon and slowly walked toward their ferocious parent.

"I've seen enough," Christian whispered. "Let's go back into the forest."

They were just about back on the trail when it happened! Neither Christian nor Winger could believe their eyes. They both immediately drew their swords and braced themselves for what was about to happen.

Chapter 24

Peggy tried to regain her balance, but it was no use. The two girls were on the ground tangled in vines which held them prisoner. It wasn't long before the beast caught up to them. Before she knew it, the beast was standing over her raising its' clawed arm preparing to strike her. She felt helpless and frustrated because she could do nothing. She looked over at Sue, feeling very sad because she never even had the opportunity to get to know her, and she felt responsible for leading her into this trap. She wanted to say goodbye to Sue and tell her how sorry she was, but Sue was looking down the path and not at her. Peggy noticed that she had a funny look on her face. It looked like she was pleading. Peggy closed her eyes tightly and awaited the blow that would end her short life.

Christian and Winger couldn't believe their eyes. In front of them were two girls flailing on the ground having just tripped over the vines that they had unloaded from the horse only hours before. One of the girls was looking at them, pleading with her eyes for them to help. The problem was that one of the beasts was rapidly approaching them.

They sprang into action and headed towards the girls. By this time the beast was standing over them about to swing its claw at the girls. Winger swung his sword with great force, striking the beast's raised arm while Christian plunged his sword into its body. The beast had been concentrating so much on its victims, who were lying helpless on the ground, that it didn't even see Christian and Winger. When it first felt the blow of the sword, the shocked beast looked up at them and attempted to swing its deadly claws at Winger and Christian, but could not. It was too late. The thrusts of Christian and Winger were fatal. The beast fell forward and almost on top of the girls, who by then, had enough presence of mind to get out of the way of the falling beast. Then it happened! The mortally wounded beast let out a roar as it fell to the ground...dead.

Christian and Winger looked at each other, then at the girls and then.... toward the clearing. It was unmistakable! The noise coming from the clearing could mean only one thing. The dragon had heard the beasts dying roar and was taking flight and more than likely would be heading in their direction. They quickly sprang into action. Christian put his finger over his lips, motioning the girls to be quiet as they helped them up. They immediately started down the path toward their campsite running as fast as they could.

Before they knew it, the dragon was flying over their heads. Only the thick canopy of the trees blocked it from seeing them. The dragon let out a blast of fire which would have fried them had it not been for the canopy. The flames, however, consumed the treetops and left the fleeing group exposed.

The dragon hovered above them and started rearing back its long neck and head ready to blast them with another burst of flame. Winger, seeing the predicament they were in, decided to take drastic action. He leapt into the air and took flight heading towards the dragon. The dragon was distracted at this unexpected event and moved its head slightly as it caught sight of Winger taking flight. It was enough to cause its fiery blast to miss Christian and the girls. Winger then flew at the dragon and swung his sword with all his might. He barely nicked the dragon's huge wing. It was just enough to irritate the gigantic monster. It turned toward Winger, who by this time having accomplished his goal, was attempting to fly away. Winger had distracted the dragon long enough for Christian and the girls to get away. The dragon let out another blast of fire, this time directly at Winger. Winger tried to evade the fiery blast but could not. It hit him, causing him to fall into the treetops and the dark forest. He had been defeated by a dragon that was a hundred times his size.

The airborne battle gave Christian and the girls time to flee deeper into the forest. As they were running down the path, Christian spotted some logs that were lying flat on the ground and had enough space under them to hide. He signaled the girls to crawl under. He followed close behind them. The girls lay under the big log and were shaking with fear. They all waited the dragon's next move. They could hear it flying above them making larger and larger circles. Finally, the noise subsided as the dragon flew further and further away.

When the dragon was far enough so that it couldn't be heard, Christian cautiously got up. He looked around and satisfied that it was safe, helped the girls to their feet. Peggy and Sue were flabbergasted. They didn't know what to say or do. First there was the beast, then Winger and Christian and then a fire-breathing dragon. Nothing in either Mustgreed's prison or the dark forest prepared them for all this.

Christian said nothing to the girls but started back in the direction they had just come to search for Winger. The girls wanted to ask Christian many questions but could sense Christian's urgency in wanting to find his companion, so they silently followed him.

Christian was frustrated. He went up and down the path and back through the freshly burnt forest where the dragon had first attacked, but to no avail. There was no sign of Winger anywhere. He walked through the forest making wider and wider circles wanting desperately to find his companion and friend, but there wasn't even the slightest trace of him. He wanted to yell out loudly and call him, but didn't dare in case the dragon was still about.

Finally, Christian sat on a log trying to figure out what to do. He couldn't believe that the dragon had killed or captured Winger. It wasn't fair. Winger was his friend. They had gone through so much together in such a short time. Christian slammed his hand against the log, on which he was sitting, with such fury that he hurt himself.

Peggy was the first to speak. "I'm sorry," she said, feeling that it was not very adequate, but it was all she could think of.

Christian looked up at her but didn't respond.

"Maybe he got away and had to fly a great distance to avoid the dragon," Sue added.

"Sure that's it," Peggy agreed, trying to sound optimistic.

"If he did get away, he will head for our campsite," Christian said trying to sound as convincing as possible not only for the girls benefit but also for his own.

"Let's go," he continued. "We'll go to the campsite. He's probably waiting for us and wondering what's taking us so long."

They made their way through the forest along the path that Christian, Winger and the horse had made during their several trips back and forth between the campsite and the clearing.

When they arrived at the campsite, Christian's heart was in his throat. He said a silent prayer that his friend would be there waiting for them. It was not to be. Winger was nowhere around.

"Maybe he went for water or something," Peggy offered still trying to keep Christian's hope alive.

They waited for hours but there was no sign of Winger. Christian was feeling sadder as each moment passed, and he realized he probably would never see his friend again. He stood up and with all the breath he could muster and yelled at the top of his lungs,

"W   I   N   G   E   R!"

He yelled so loud that all the birds in the area fluttered and flew and cawed, and all the animals squawked and ran up and down trees and across the ground of the dark forest, but there was no response from Winger.

Chapter 25

Christian and the two girls spent the night at the campsite without speaking much to each other. It was obvious to the girls that Christian did not want to talk because he was very upset and worried about Winger. The girls kept themselves busy with the horses and enjoyed petting and feeding them.

The next morning they woke up to a bright and sunny day. Christian had a very restless night. He already missed Winger terribly. He knew he had to carry on because that was what Winger would want him to do, and besides, he wanted more than ever to kill the dragon. It was personal now. He would avenge Winger, but how? With Winger gone how could he finish the gigantic bow and arrow by himself? He had to think. He had to force the thoughts of Winger out of his mind for a while so that he could accomplish his quest. Then he would have time to mourn for his lost friend.

The girls ate a hearty breakfast, but Christian just picked at his food. Finally, he looked at the girls and introduced himself. For the first time they learned the name of the person who saved them.

The girls felt a little awkward as they introduced themselves and started to tell Christian about the other children and the cave. Then they told him about Mustgreed and the drones and the horrible conditions at the labor camps where they were held prisoner. The more they talked the better they felt. Christian began to listen intently, and he also felt a little better. For the first time, his quest in the dark forest started to take form. It was no longer a dream. Standing in front of him was living proof of what the wizard had told Winger and him.

Then it was Christian's turn. He told the girls about his quest and the beasts he had killed and the gigantic bow and arrow they were making and how they had been preparing to kill the dragon so that they could free the boys and girls from Mustgreed and lead them safely back to the village. The girls were very excited to hear Christian's plans. Once again visions of her father and family flashed through Sue's head.

They decided that they should go to the cave to let the other children know that they were alright and to introduce Christian.

Christian felt that he could gain a great deal of intelligence from the children about the camp and Mustgreed.

The trip didn't take long at all. They took the horses with Christian on one horse and Peggy and Sue riding double on the other.

When they arrived, the log was in front of the entrance just as the girls had described. The children inside the cave were so excited, that after they lifted the log they almost dropped it in their zeal to see the girls and Christian. Marie ran to the horse that was carrying the girls and hugged Sue's leg. Sue jumped off the horse and threw her arms around Marie.

"I was so afraid the beast got you," Marie said.

"It's a long story," Sue responded as they walked hand in hand inside the cave, leading the horse in behind them.

The other children gathered around Peggy and Sue greeting them heartily. They cautiously looked around at Christian and the horses. Christian introduced himself to the other children, and Tom, once again acting as spokesman for the group, introduced everyone.

The day was spent talking to each other. The children were telling their stories, and Christian was telling his right up to the battle with the dragon and the disappearance of Winger. Christian explained the plans to build the gigantic bow and arrow in order to kill the dragon.

"I guess I can forget about that now. Without Winger I'll never be able to finish it," Christian said deep in thought.

"We can help," Tom volunteered.

"Thanks, but it is very tough work. It requires heavy lifting to get everything in place," Christian responded.

"What we don't have in size we can make up in numbers," Tom quickly answered getting excited at the prospect of helping Christian kill the dragon.

"I don't know; I'm not sure it will work," Christian answered pondering the suggestion. "I guess we could still use the horses for the very heavy work, but lifting the arrow into place, that'll take a lot of strength. I just don't know..." Christian's voice trailed off as he became deep in thought trying to figure out if it were possible. Then he said, "It might be worth a try, but everyone would have to understand how dangerous it will be. Peggy and Sue can testify to the dragon's awesome power".

"Sure, we can help; you'll see," Tom said, his voice full of excitement. "You'll be surprised at how strong and resourceful we are, after all, each of us survived the camp, escaped Mustgreed and have been doing okay here on our own."

"Okay," Christian said, "I'll take some of you to the clearing tomorrow and we'll give it a try. I guess there is strength in numbers. Remember though, we have to be very quiet if the dragon is there. We can only work when he's away. This will give us only limited amounts of time we can work. Now that I think of it, we can use some of you to keep an eye on the clearing and warn us if the dragon returns, and some can stay in the campsite Winger and I had. "Yes," he exclaimed, "we can use that as a temporary stop over between here and the clearing".

Christian was getting more and more enthusiastic as he made plans for the next day. He could see that Tom and the other children were excited as well, talking away with each other and mimicking how they would work hard and beat that old dragon. Some of the children pretended to throw spears at a make believe dragon, while others pretended to be the dragon and fall onto the ground, dying of their imaginary wounds. It was fun. At last they had a plan and something to do besides just survive in a cave from day to day. They felt that this might lead to them being able to help free the other children who were still being held prisoner by Mustgreed.

Christian unsaddled the horses and took the armor off them in preparation for sleep. The children helped with the equipment and enjoyed petting the horses and feeding them.
After a while, the cave quieted down with everyone trying to fall asleep. But thoughts of seeing the other children, and perhaps even leaving the dark forest and getting home, made sleeping almost impossible that night.

The next morning there was an air of excitement in the cave. The children busied themselves with their chores but had only one thing on their minds. They wanted to see the dragon and show Christian the prison where Mustgreed was still holding their friends.

"You had better select about ten children to come with us," Christian told Tom.

Tom looked dejected. How was he going to pick children to come with him while the others would be left behind? He realized that he had to leave some of them back to ensure that the log was left in place so that no monsters would be waiting for them inside the cave when they got back, and besides, too many children may make it difficult to keep them quiet when they neared the clearing and the dragon.

He picked seven children. Along with himself, Peggy and Sue had a total of ten. He promised the others that they could come with them tomorrow. Again, Marie was not picked, and she was to be left behind in the cave. She felt sad but understood that she had an important job to do…helping with the log to secure the safe haven.

Christian and the children started out, went a short distance and then waited outside the cave for the log to be lowered into place. After they saw that the job was complete, they made their way down the path that would lead them to the dragon and some events that they were definitely not prepared for.

Chapter 26

They slowly made their way down the narrow path. Christian led the way on foot holding the reins of his horse on which two children were riding. The other children followed in single file behind them with Tom at the rear. The dark forest seemed more ominous than ever. It was pitch black in spots, and the children would have been very scared had it not been for Christian leading the way.

After what seemed to be a long time, they finally came to the campsite which was bathed in warm sunlight. They felt much better in the campsite and began to chatter among themselves. Tom chastised them for talking loudly, but Christian explained that they were far enough from the clearing and the dragon not to be heard. However, he did tell them to whisper so they got used to speaking in low tones and would have less of a chance of slipping when they did get to the clearing.

Christian told Tom to select two children to leave at the campsite and care for the horses when they were not needed. These children could then rotate with the others if they were tired and needed a rest. Christian explained that the clearing was only about fifteen minutes away by foot, and that they couldn't get lost because there was only one path which he and Winger had made between the campsite and the clearing.

They decided to spend an hour or so at the campsite and have some fruit they had brought with them from the cave for lunch. After eating, Christian, Tom, Peggy, Sue and five of the other children started for the clearing. Before leaving the campsite, Christian cautioned them about talking loudly or leaving the path. He especially warned them about the area where the dragon had consumed the canopy of the trees with its fire. He warned that they would be exposed if the dragon was flying overhead. He told them that if that happened they should try to remain perfectly still so that, with a little luck, the dragon may not see them.

They slowly approached the clearing. When he thought they were close enough, Christian signaled the children to get down on their hands and knees and crawl to the clearing.

The dragon was there. It was lying down at the other end of the clearing where it usually rested. The children were awed by the size of it. Up until this time it was just a game and imaginary to the children, but there it was. It was as big as a house and very scary. Christian signaled the children to crawl away from the clearing. When they were far enough away, they laid down in the grass where there were still some rays of sunshine coming through the dark forest near the clearing. The children began to whisper to each other, but this time there was no giggling. They had seen the huge dragon, and they were scared.

After an hour had passed with no movement from the dragon, Christian decided to show the children the place where he and Winger had started the huge bow. Once again, he cautioned them to be quiet as they crawled toward the clearing. This time they were closer to where the dragon was lying.

When they arrived at the edge of the clearing where the bow was, the children could see the work that Christian and Winger had completed. Using hand signals along with drawing diagrams on the ground, Christian gave them the concept of how he hoped it would work. He then had them crawl to the spot where the giant arrow was being hewn from a tree. The children began to grasp the plan and how it should work, but Tom had some serious questions. He decided to wait until later to ask.

A few hours passed, and the dragon did not move. Christian decided to call it a day and head back to the campsite. The children were disappointed that they did not see the dragon fly and that they did not get to do any work on the weapon.

They returned to the campsite and then went on to the cave. The children in the cave were surprised to see them back so quickly. They thought that they would be out at least until nightfall. Christian and the children waited for the log to be lifted and then entered the cave.

After dinner that night, Tom starting asking questions of Christian. "How will we keep the arrow pointed at the dragon?" he asked.

"I intend to make a stanchion, perhaps out of a log. It will have to be the right height so that when the arrow rests on it, it will be pointed above the dragon. I think we'll have to construct it so that it is elevated in the front of the arrow because the log or arrow will be so big and heavy that it is bound to come down quicker than I would like. What I intend to do is fire one arrow when the dragon is not there to ensure that we have the right height, and it will go far enough with enough force to do the job," Christian responded.

"Does the dragon always rest in the same area?" was Tom's next question.

"Yes, all the times we saw it, it always stayed in about the same area," Christian answered. "We will be able to move the shot to the right or left by moving the horse at the angle we want it to go. Of course we can't move it too much because of the trees we are using for a bow."

Christian suddenly realized that all the children had been intently listening to their conversation and had gathered around him and Tom. He smiled at them and said, "Tomorrow we'll have a better day. I can feel it".

The next morning they started out again. The children were full of enthusiasm.

Once again they stopped at the campsite but did not stay for lunch. They left two children back at the campsite and continued down the path toward the clearing. As they walked their thoughts were interrupted by the sound of large wings flapping. Christian quickly motioned for all the children to get down. It wasn't necessary because they had already ducked under bushes or whatever they could find to hide themselves. The sound was so loud that it had to be the dragon. There was a collective sigh of relief when the noise became fainter and fainter until it was completely gone.

Christian motioned for everyone to get up. He led them directly to the clearing where the trees were. He looked around just to make sure the dragon was gone. He told Tom to send two children back to get a horse because he was going to attempt to move the arrow-shaped log from where it had been cut to the trees that would act as its bow.

Christian busied himself hacking away at branches on the tree trunk that would serve as an arrow. He had Tom and some of the children retrieve the vines that had been left on the path and had given Peggy and Sue a hard time by ensnaring them when they were fleeing from the beast. He had also assigned one of the children to keep an eye on the clearing in the event that the dragon came back, and they did not hear it because of the noise of the chopping.

By midafternoon the tree trunk was ready. Christian tied some vines on it. The other end of the vines was fastened to the horse's saddlehorn. He led the horse to the bow and then untied the makeshift arrow.

The next step would be to make a stanchion of some sort in order to rest the arrow on it. The stanchion would have to be high enough to elevate the front of the arrow. Christian explained to the children what would be needed, and they spread out in search for the proper log. After a few false alarms, two of the children found one that looked to be about the right size and shape.

Once again, Christian tied some vines on the log and began to drag it to the trees/bow. The log was extremely heavy, and the horse struggled against the vines tugging with all its strength in order to drag it. The children tried to help by pushing on the back of the log.

At last they made it to the clearing where the bow was.

Christian didn't like what he had to do next. In order to properly place the log, which would act as a stanchion for the arrow, he would have to lead the horse into the clearing. He motioned for the children to stay back as he led the horse into the clearing, exposing him and the horse.

Then they heard it! It was the unmistakable flapping of the dragon's wings. Everyone dropped down low in the brush as the children, who were assigned to keep watch over the clearing, came running.

"It's back, its back," they said breathlessly.

Christian said nothing but signaled them to get down.

Christian was in a quandary. He and the horse were in the clearing, and the dragon was circling overhead. If he tried to lead the horse back into the forest, the motion might get the attention of the dragon, and that would be certain death, especially since the horse was still tied to the vines and the log and, therefore, could not move quickly. If he tried to run for it and the dragon saw him, it would probably shoot a fiery blast at him and besides him, the children would probably be harmed.

He decided to try to make a run for it. He jumped on the horse and tugged on its reins to get it to turn and head back into the forest.

It was too late.

The dragon saw the movement in the clearing and decided to come lower and take a look at what it was.
Christian struggled to get the horse to move faster, and at the same time motioned for the children to run deeper into the forest.

The vines which were fastened to the horse's saddle were pulled taught and had caught Christian's leg forcing it hard against the saddle and the side of the horse.

The horse sensed the danger that was approaching and tried to rear up on its hind legs but, because of the vines, could not. It let out a whinny which caused the dragon to zero in on him and his struggling rider.

The dragon headed right for them, then reared its ugly head back and prepared to let go of a fiery blast which would destroy both of them.

Chapter 27

Christian looked over his shoulder and saw that the children had gone deep enough into the forest that they were no longer visible. Then he looked up, and what he saw frightened him. The dragon was about to let go of his deadly fiery blast. Christian knew he had only seconds to act. His leg was still jammed against the side of the horse making it impossible for him to jump off. The horse's nostrils flared as he struggled fiercely to move, but the heavy log had caught on the trunk of a tree held him back. This caused the vines to strain and become even tighter against Christian's leg. They started to cut into Christian's leg, which was jammed between the saddle of the horse and under the vine, causing him severe pain.

Christian pulled out his sword and with a wide arc slashed at the vines over the back of the horse. The vines were severed with the first stroke of the sharp sword causing the horse to lunge forward almost dislodging Christian from the saddle. The rapid, jerking, forward motion was enough to bring them just out of range of the fiery blast which consumed the foliage on the ground and the log and the vines where Christian and his horse had just left a split second ago.

The dragon reared back for another shot, but by this time Christian was galloping at full speed. He reentered the dark forest at the opposite side of where he had left and where the children were. The horse crashed into the forest causing bushes to flail on each side of them. The horse's armor protected him from injury as they forged a new path into the foreboding forest.
Overhead Christian could hear the dragon, and then the forest lit up.

It happened about a hundred yards behind them where the dragon struck again in an attempt to find them. Christian kept pushing the horse onward, but the horse needed no encouragement. The dragon provided all the incentive necessary.

At last it was quiet. Christian slowed the horse to a normal walk and listened for any sound that would indicate that the dragon was about. He heard nothing. After a while he decided it was safe to stop and rest. Both he and the horse were exhausted. He only allowed himself a few minutes rest as he was worried about the children he had left on the other side of the clearing. He remounted, turned around and was heading back down the path they had just forged through the thick dark forest.

When he was near the clearing, he hesitated. He decided to tie the reins of the horse on a nearby tree and crawl to the edge of the clearing to see if he could spot what the dragon was up to. As he approached, to his surprise, the dragon was almost in front of him. He then realized that he had entered the forest almost at the exact spot where the dragon usually laid down. Luckily, the dragon was facing the other way and had no inkling that Christian was behind him.

Christian surveyed the huge back of the dragon. Its skin looked like green metal. It towered way above Christian. For a second, Christian was tempted to take his sword and stab at it but knew that it would only aggravate this monster and probably get him killed in response. He quietly crawled back to where he left the horse, untied it and figured out that they would have to find a different way back to the children. It was slow going. The forest was thick and unyielding. As soon as he felt and was far enough away that the dragon could not hear him, he took out his sword and started to cut a path. It was difficult, and he had to rest several times.

He finally came upon the path that they had used between the campsite and the clearing. He decided to go to the clearing first in case the children had decided to stay in that area and wait for him. They were not around, so Christian mounted his horse and slowly rode to the campsite.

When he arrived he was surprised to find it empty. It was getting dark rapidly, so he decided to stay at the campsite for the night. He knew that it would do no good to continue his search as he would probably end up getting lost in the dark. He could only hope that the children decided to go back to the cave and were safe.

After all the work of the day and the excitement of dealing with the dragon, Christian was very weary. It took all the strength he could muster just to take the saddle and armor off the horse. He was totally exhausted and practically fell onto the ground sound asleep.

Chapter 28

The children were frightened at the sight of the dragon and the noise of its powerful wings as it flew over their heads. They hid themselves at the edge of the clearing as they watched Christian and the horse struggle against the weight of the log they were dragging. When Christian signaled them to run further into the forest, they did so without hesitation. They ran as fast as their young legs would take them.

The edge of the clearing lit up with fire as the dragon let go of a burst of fire at Christian. The children were far enough not to get burnt, but they did feel the intense heat as they ran. In fact, it made them run all the faster. They kept going all the way to the campsite, where they laid down trying to catch their breath, all the while keeping a sharp ear for the unmistakable flapping noise of the dragon.

After they had rested and caught their breath, they began to talk about what had just taken place and what they should do next.

"I think we should wait here for Christian," Peggy volunteered.

"I agree," Sue said while picking leaves off her dress.

"I don't know about that," Tom said deep in thought. "What if the dragon got Christian, and he doesn't return?"

"What if he's injured and is making his way back here and needs our help?" Peggy answered.
"Okay," Tom responded. "Let's wait here for a while, but before it starts getting dark, I vote we make our way back to the cave."

"I think we should wait as long as possible," Sue retorted.

"You don't want to be stuck out here all night do you? Don't forget the monsters that are roaming around and the dragon is out there somewhere," Tom responded.

The thoughts of the dragon and the monsters were enough to convince everyone that Tom was right. It was decided that they would wait in the campsite as long as they could, but as soon as they thought it was getting dark, they would head for the cave as quickly as they could.

"In the meantime, let's rest and store up some energy in case we have to make a run for it," Tom advised.

All the children agreed, and they laid down on the ground. It was decided that they would take turns resting and keeping an eye out for the monsters and, hopefully, Christian.

They waited for a few hours, and then decided it was starting to get dark, and they would make a dash for the cave. Tom led the way with the children following. Darkness was coming on fast in the already dark forest, so Tom started to run. He decided to put Peggy in front of the group because then he could bring up the rear and make sure none of the children fell behind as it was almost black in the forest by now.

They had started out too late! Peggy stopped in her tracks. She couldn't see ahead of her, and she was afraid she would get off the path and be lost forever. Tom went forward to see why she stopped. He made sure the children gathered in a tight group and then pondered what they should do next.

He didn't have long to think. Fate made the decision for him. Directly in front of them was this huge silhouette of something. There was no way to get around it or escape.

The children let out a gasp and huddled together.

They were finished, Tom thought. Maybe I can attack it, and when it kills me it'll be satisfied and let the other children go. He took a deep breath and ran forward to what he thought was certain death.

Chapter 29

Tom ran directly at the figure hurling his body as hard as he could. It was useless. He bounced off the figure and fell onto the ground. All of a sudden, he felt two strong hands lift him off the ground and stand him on his feet.

"Err...err..." Tom didn't know what to say or do. He thought about kicking at the figure but knew it would have no effect.

"What is your problem?" the large figure said. "I am not going to hurt you or the other children. Who are you, and where did you come from?"

"We... er... we're with the knight, and the dragon attacked and we ran and the knight....er...er I don't know.. er...er...," Tom said stammering at this unexpected occurrence.

"Knight...you mean Christian?" He asked hoping that was who the boy was talking about.

"Yes, sir...yes, Christian. How did you know?" Tom asked relieved. "You.... you must be Winger," Tom happily concluded. "Christian told us all about you."

"Yes I am," Winger answered.

"What are you doing out here in the dark forest?" Winger asked.

"We were on our way to the cave when it got dark, and we were afraid we were going to get lost," Tom explained.

"Is the cave down this path?" Winger inquired.

"Yes, but we can't see; it's pitch black," Tom answered.

"I can see," Winger responded, confident that his owl eyes could pierce the darkness. "I'll take you down the path. Have the children form a line each holding on to the one in front so that we don't get separated."

Tom quickly complied with Winger's request and excitedly told the children that it was Winger, the same Winger that Christian told them about.

The children were relieved at this turn of events and grabbed on to each other's hands and in turn Tom's, who held tightly onto Winger's hand.

They were only about a hundred yards from the cave, but in the darkness the children had no way of knowing they were so close. When they arrived, they called to the children inside who lifted the log and then lowered it after they all entered. When the children saw Winger they didn't know what to think until Tom explained that it was Winger, the very same Winger that Christian had told them about.

Winger looked terrible. Peggy and Sue, who were saved by Winger and Christian from the beast in the forest a couple of days earlier, barely recognized him.

Winger could see the expression in the eyes of the children, so he started to explain how he had taken flight in order to distract the dragon so that Christian, Peggy and Sue could get away. Unfortunately for him, he explained, the dragon's fiery blast came a little too close and caused him to dive directly into the dark forest, and he crashed through the trees and eventually hit the hard ground and was knocked unconscious. He figured he had been out for quite a while. When he woke up he was in terrible pain and could hardly move. His wing was singed by the dragon's blast, and it had taken all his energy and time just to make his way to the path where he bumped into the children.

"I'm still sore, and I feel exhausted," he said.

"Why don't you lay down, and we'll get you something to eat?" Tom asked.

"I will, but first I would like to know where Christian is."

The children, who were with Christian when the dragon attacked, looked at each other. No one wanted to tell Winger about his friend and the dragon getting him. After all, no one really could have escaped that fiery blast.

First, Peggy and Sue explained how they and Christian evaded the dragon the day Winger was hurt. After that, they went looking for him. When they couldn't find him, they made their way back to the cave.

Once again, Tom was to be the spokesman for the group.

"The last time we saw him was at the clearing where the dragon was. He signaled us to get away as the dragon was heading in our direction. The dragon let go of a blast that almost got us, and I don't know if...if Christian got away. Then we ran as fast as we could and eventually made our way to the campsite. We waited for him,...but..but… he didn't show up," Tom said looking at Winger to see if he could grasp his reaction to the events of the day.

Winger started to get up.

"I have to go see if he's alright," he said, but then fell back down too exhausted to move.

By this time, the children bought some food for him to eat, but

Winger had already fallen asleep.

They tried to make him as comfortable as possible.

The children who had been with Tom that day were also exhausted, and everyone decided to get to sleep so that they could start out early the next morning to see if they could find Christian.

Chapter 30

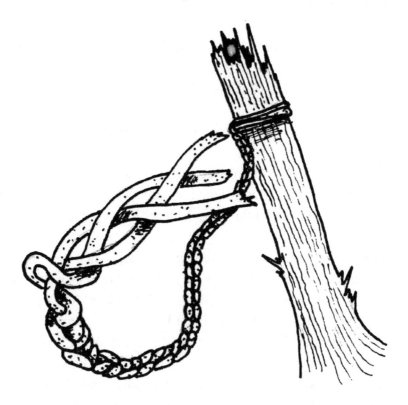

The next morning, Winger and the children were awakened by shouts coming from outside the cave.

"Hey in there, open up, lift the log."

It was Christian sitting on his horse with a huge smile on his face.

The children ran for the vines to lift up the log and let him in. They were all excited because they thought the dragon had surely killed him.

When Winger and Christian saw each other they embraced and jumped for joy.

"I...I thought you were dead for sure," Christian said to Winger.

"I thought you were dead, too," Winger responded.

"We thought you were both dead," Tom added.

They sat and told and retold the events of the last few days to each other while the children listened intently. They were so happy to be together again after thinking that they had lost each other.

Most of the morning was taken up with talk. Then they got very serious and began to plan how they were going to take care of the dragon. Both Christian and Winger felt that they had a personal quest to get that dragon for what it had done to them. They were more determined than ever. It was decided that Christian and Winger would continue with the building of the bow and arrow. They decided that the children would only come as far as the campsite and could work on stringing new vines into a large rope for the bow to replace the one the dragon had burnt.

The rest of the day was spent eating and resting so that Winger could recuperate a little longer, nurse his burnt wing, and get some more of his strength back.

The next morning they got up early and were raring to go. After a quick breakfast, they started out. Christian was in the lead; five of the children were in the middle, and Winger was bringing up the rear. When they arrived at the campsite, they cautioned the children to keep watch for the dragon. Then, Christian and Winger cut some vines that they were sure could be turned into the type of rope they needed and gave it to the children. They explained to them once more how the vines should be entwined to make the strong rope needed to do the job.

Christian and Winger then left the children and proceeded to the clearing. When they arrived, they crawled to the edge and were relieved to find that the dragon was not there. They immediately went looking for another log to act as the stanchion for the front of the arrow. This time they decided to make it higher as the dragon would probably hear or see them, and they would have to get a shot at it as it was attacking them. They knew this would be extremely dangerous but figured it was probably the only way they would get a clear shot at it.

It didn't take too long to find the proper size lo, and this time they tied it to the two horses and had it in place in no time at all.

All was quiet...still no sign of the dragon.

They then lifted the giant arrow so that its front was resting on the stanchion with the back on the ground.

All quiet....still no sign of the dragon.

They decided to make the second arrow. They located the right size tree and cut it down and fashioned it into the right size. They sharpened a point to it and then bought it to the bow and sat it on the ground next to it.

All quiet....still no sign of the dragon.

They returned to the campsite and the children. They had finished the vine/rope. Christian and Winger inspected it and tried it for strength by pulling on it.

"This is great," Christian said.

"Just what the doctor ordered," Winger added.

"You stay here, and Winger and I will rig it up. We'll be back later," Christian said.

They returned to the clearing.

All quiet....still no sign of the dragon.

They rigged the vines and decided to test their invention.

They tied the vines to the log/arrow and then to the horn on the saddle. Winger led the horse back, and it strained against the vine. The force the horse exerted bent the top of the trees and the arrow came back.

Christian looked at Winger and smiled.

"Let her go," Winger said.

Christian took out his sword and cut the vine. The force of the trees repelling back caused the arrow to be hurled into space. It landed about seventy-five yards away.

All quiet....still no sign of the dragon.

"I'll go get it," volunteered Winger.

"No, you're still a little weak. I'll get it."

Before Winger could object, Christian was on his way into the clearing galloping as fast as he could.

Winger busied himself setting up the next arrow and attaching more vines.

All quiet....still no sign of the dragon.

Christian tied some vines onto the log and then on the saddlehorn and started dragging it back to the bow.

It was unmistakable! The flapping noise had to be the dragon. Christian urged the horse onward as it struggled against the weight. They made it. They got to the bow just as the dragon flew overhead.

Christian and Winger rapidly worked on placing the arrow on the stanchion and tying the vines to the bow and then to the horn of the saddle on Winger's horse.

The dragon went to its usual landing place about a hundred yards away. Christian and Winger realized that they couldn't shoot that far with any force. A decision had to be made! Winger once again led his horse back, straining against the vines and bending the arrow back.

Christian mounted his horse, drew his sword and headed right for the dragon, yelling as he charged.

The dragon, who was first startled and then annoyed by the intruder, immediately took flight. Christian turned his horse around and headed back to the bow and prepared arrow hoping the dragon would follow.

The dragon was right behind and above him. Christian headed for the bow which was stretched to the limit and cut the vines causing the arrow to fly.

It was too late..... Winger thought*.....the arrow would never strike the dragon. The dragon would be past it by the time the arrow got there and it would fall behind it, missing it entirely.*
And he was right.

Chapter 31

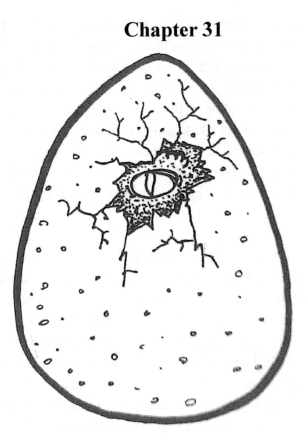

The arrow was going to miss the dragon!

Then the miracle happened.

The dragon reared back to fire a blast at Christian and Winger who were sitting near the huge bow. In order for the dragon to fire its blast, it had to stop its flight. It reared back to have sufficient force for the fire to travel the distance necessary to incinerate its foe. The stopping of the dragon's forward momentum was long enough for the arrow to find its mark. The giant arrow struck the dragon in its neck. It was not a killing blow but certainly seriously injured the dragon. The fiery blast that was sure to come and consume Christian and Winger turned out to be a trickle due to the blow of the arrow. The dragon fluttered in confusion and pain. It roared and tried to dislodge the arrow with its grotesque claws but could not. Finally, in desperation, it flew into some trees and the arrow came out but not without taking its toll on the dragon. Green blood from the dragon splattered everywhere. The dragon fluttered and sputtered around a little more and then landed in the clearing next to where Christian and Winger were busy preparing their next arrow.

The adrenaline was surging in Christian and Winger's veins as they worked furiously at their desperate attempt to prepare the arrow for firing before the dragon could get them. The dragon was so big that it towered over them as it lay on the ground almost on top of them. It growled and tried to blast them with fire but to no avail. The first arrow had choked off its ability to shoot fire. The dragon then attempted to get to its feet so that it could fall forward and crush its gallant adversaries. It was so close to them that Christian could feel its breath. He and Winger worked furiously placing the arrow and tying the vines to the horse as the dragon once again attempted to move toward them in order to crush them. Finally, their work preparing the arrow was complete, and Winger started the horse back to put strain on the bow with the arrow at the ready position to fire. The dragon was almost on top of them when Christian cut the vine sending the arrow at point blank range into the chest of the dragon. The dragon let out an ear splitting howl, then convulsed in an attempt to dislodge the arrow. Then it fell over backwards. It thrashed about for a short period of time and, at last, let out its final breath and died.

Christian and Winger cautiously approached the dragon. They were afraid that the dragon might flail again and crush them. Christian took out his sword and thrust it into the dragon, but it did not move. At last, they were convinced that the dragon was dead. They had defeated their most formidable foe. Out of nervousness and habit, they retreated back to the forest in order to get a little further away from the dragon, still not fully trusting it was dead.

Then Christian and Winger fell on the ground relieved and exhausted. All the strength had been taken out of them by the brief but fierce struggle. All they wanted to do was rest. They laid there for a while with the huge dead dragon close by. They looked at the dragon and then at each other and began to giggle. They we so relieved that the few minutes of sheer terror had past and that they had been successful in their quest to kill the dragon. They felt giddy. Then they laughed and laughed and laughed and rolled around the ground until their sides hurt them.

In the meantime, the children had heard the dying howl of the dragon and became frightened. They didn't know what had happened or what to do. They decided that they should look for Christian and Winger. They slowly and cautiously approached the clearing. As they arrived near the clearing, they heard all the laughter and didn't know what to make of it.

It was a funny sight, Christian and Winger rolling around on the ground, laughing and giggling. Because it was such a funny sight and so catching, the children started laughing too. Then Tom turned and saw the dead dragon lying on the ground almost next to them and stopped laughing as a shudder ran through his body. One by one, the children saw the dragon and also stopped laughing.

137

After a while, when everything calmed down, they decided to head back to the cave. On the way back, the children, who were happy over the dragon's death, played and kidded around with each other.

When they arrived, the children who had remained behind lifted the entrance log so they could all enter. Inside the children chattered away telling about the huge dragon that Christian and Winger had slain. The children begged Christian and Winger to tell them all about the battle with the dragon. They were tired and didn't feel like talking, but the children were so excited and insistent that they couldn't say no. They told the children the entire story from the beginning of the battle to the gruesome end. The children became even more excited and made Christian and Winger promise to take the ones that weren't there to see the dragon in the clearing tomorrow.

That night, the children had trouble falling asleep because of all the excitement. Christian and Winger had no problem sleeping since they were exhausted from all that had happened to them that day.

The next morning, after breakfast, the children kept asking Christian and Winger when they would leave to see the dragon. After a while, they saddled their horses, and when the log was lifted, started out on the path with the other children who had not seen the dragon.

The day seemed a lot brighter, even in the dark forest. The birds seemed to be singing louder, and the noises of the forest seemed just a little more friendly. They guessed it was because the dragon was no longer a threat, and they were well on their way to accomplishing their goal of freeing the children.

First, they went to the campsite and showed the children where they had set up camp and where the other children made the vines and waited for them. The children enjoyed looking around and being able to visualize what had happened. Up to that point, it had been just a story.

After a while, they set out for the clearing. They ambled along the trail, and Christian pointed out where the dragon had burnt the treetops with its fiery blast. He showed them where Peggy and Sue were trapped by the vines that he and Winger had left on the trail. They motioned with their arms as to how the children were trapped and how the monster was almost on top of them when they spotted the girls and saved them. The children enjoyed the story even more this time.

Soon, they left the clearing. First, Christian showed the children the bow that was used so effectively to down the dragon. He explained how it worked and how Winger would lead the horse back and how he would cut the vines letting the arrow fly. Then, the children turned and looked around.

There it was. It looked even more huge and menacing lying there, green blood still oozing from its neck forming a ghoulish puddle on the ground. Protruding from the dragon's chest was the arrow that Christian and Winger had dispatched it with the day before. It was as ugly as ever. The children wanted a better look at the dragon. They cautiously made their way closer and closer. The laughter and playing that had taken place earlier that day faded as they realized the immense size and obvious ferociousness of the dragon. It towered over them even lying on its side. It was about the size of a two-story house.

What they saw then sickened them and struck fear in their hearts. They all started to scream.

Christian and Winger had remained back a few paces looking at the large bow when they heard the children's screams. They raced toward the clearing.

"What's wrong?" Winger asked in response to the screams.

"I don't know," Christian answered.

Christian and Winger both drew their swords and ran as fast as they could into the clearing, hoping that they would not be too late.

When Christian and Winger ran into the clearing they were not prepared for what they saw. Even the children's screams did not foretell how gruesome the sight would be. The children came running past them away from the clearing and into the forest. Christian could see that their faces were etched with fear as they ran by them.

Then, Winger and Christian saw them. Directly in front of them were the red-eyed monsters, about seven of them, the offspring of the dragon. What they were doing revolted both Christian and Winger. They were eating the dragon! They had green blood all over their faces. The children's screams made the monsters stop what they were doing to look up. They obviously did not like being disturbed during their meal. Then, they saw Christian and Winger and attacked flailing away with their razor sharp claws.

The ensuing battle didn't take very long. As before, when fighting with them, they were too stupid to realize that they were no match for the sharp swords of Christian and Winger, who parried and moved from side to side avoiding their blows while striking fatal sword strokes at them. Had they been a little older and had they developed wings, it might have been a different story. Before long they were all dead.

Christian and Winger looked at each other and decided to walk around the huge dead dragon to make sure there were no more monsters on the other side. After warning the children to stay near the edge of the clearing but in the protection of the forest, Christian walked in one direction and Winger in the other so that they wouldn't miss them if there were anymore. There weren't.
"I guess we got them all," Winger said, meeting up with Christian.
"I sure hope so. I don't want any of them sneaking up behind us some night," Christian responded. "Let's go back and get the children."

The children were hiding at the edge of the clearing behind some thick shrubbery. They were very glad to see Christian and Winger and did not want to linger near the dead dragon or the clearing any longer.

Once again, they formed a single file line and headed back to the cave.

When they arrived, the log was lifted, and they entered. The children, who had accompanied Christian and Winger, couldn't wait to tell the others the gruesome details of the monsters and the dead dragon. After all the talk, dinner was prepared, and before long it was time to go to bed.

Chapter 32

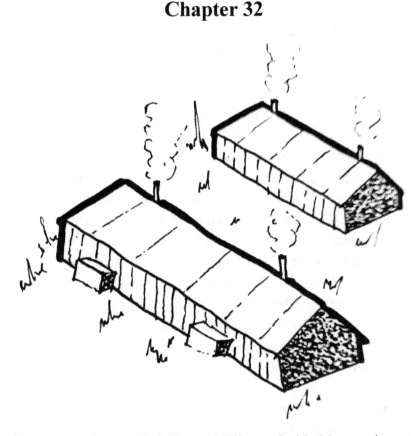

The next morning, Christian and Winger decided it was time to start their attempt to rescue the children from Mustgreed. *The best way to start*, they thought, *would be to question each of the children in order to gain as much knowledge as they could about the camp, drones and Mustgreed.*

It took most of the day. The children tried to be as helpful as possible, but it turned out that they were isolated from one another. They were all treated pretty badly, and they all lived in barrack-type housing. What was most helpful was that they had kept regular hourly schedules. They were taken in groups to work in the mines, which were quite a distance from the barracks. It took about fifteen to twenty minutes to get there. They were always escorted by drones and were never allowed to roam freely about the camp. Meals were sparse and either eaten in a mess hall, or sometimes food would be bought to the barracks by some of the children who worked the kitchen detail. They were almost always watched by the drones and could never leave the barracks unless escorted. As for Mustgreed, he was rarely seen, and he was always accompanied by soldiers dressed in battle gear and carrying weapons, usually spears. The children were also fairly sure that they carried swords and shields. They appeared to be well-disciplined and probably would die if ordered to do so by Mustgreed. Unfortunately, the children did not know how many soldiers there were, because they never saw them all at once. They had no idea where the soldiers lived. They did assume it was close to the camp, because anytime an alarm was sounded, the soldiers would arrive in minutes.

Christian and Winger decided that they would get an early start the next morning and visit the camp. They decided that they should not take any of the children, except for Tom who would show them the way. He could explain the camp to them as they moved around the edge of the dark forest. One thing they knew they had in their favor was that the drones were afraid of the dark forest and probably would not enter it. The drones did have an alarm system, however, that would immediately bring other drones and either Mustgreed or some of his soldiers.

The next morning, Christian and Winger prepared themselves to leave the cave and head for the camp. They decided not to take the horses because they felt that they would only look at the camp from the cover of the dark forest. The horses would only be in the way.

After the log was lifted, the three of them started out with Tom pointing the way. They made their way down paths which Christian marked either by placing stones on the ground in the shape of an arrow or notching trees. In this way he felt that he and Winger could find their way back and forth and would not have to endanger Tom by bringing him with them.

It wasn't long before they arrived at the edge of the camp where the children were being held prisoner. They peered out of the dark forest and surveyed the camp. It was just as the children had described, very austere. It resembled a prison with its stark barracks with grey roofs and unpainted wood siding.

Tom pointed out the different buildings that he was aware of.

"Over there is the kitchen and the mess hall," he motioned toward a building.

"Where is the mine that you were forced to work in?" Christian asked.

"Down that way, beyond the mess hall and up the hill," Tom pointed in the direction.

Just then, a drone came out of the mess hall and was followed by a child who was carrying a bag as big as he was. The boy struggled with the bag as the drone took off the garbage pail lid. The boy was finally able to let go of the bag, dropping it into the pail, obviously relieved at not having to struggle with the weight of the bag any longer.

"Those drones do not look very tough to me," Winger said. "They're not very much taller than the children. They're about five-feet tall and built like gorillas and extremely stocky."

"Are they all like that?" Winger asked Tom.

"Yes," Tom responded. "They all look like that. Some of them okay, but some are very cruel," Tom continued.

Just then, the drone they had been watching shoved the boy into the mess hall.

Winger was on his feet and ready to go after him when Christian stopped him.

"Not yet," Christian said. "Our time will come, but this is not it."

Christian then turned his attention to Tom.

"Are Mustgreed and his soldiers built the same way?" he inquired.

"No," Tom answered, "they are as tall as you are and look very tough and mean."

"Okay," Christian responded. "Why don't you go back to the cave? We will circle the camp and see what else there is. Perhaps, if we are lucky, we will run across Mustgreed. By the way, are

Mustgreed and his soldiers afraid of the dark forest?"

"I don't know," Tom responded. "I never saw them go into the dark forest, but while I was in the camp they had no reason to."

"Why can't I go along with you?" Tom asked.

"We don't know what we'll meet up with. We may bump into Mustgreed, and it might get dangerous," Christian answered.

"I won't get in the way; I promise," Tom pleaded.

"No, we can't take that chance," Christian answered firmly. "Go back to the cave, and we'll see you later."

Tom shrugged his shoulders, obviously disappointed, and slowly turned around towards the path that would take him back to the cave.

Christian and Winger continued around the edge of the camp making sure they stayed in the cover of the dark forest. Before long, they were beyond the mess hall and going parallel to a large clearing which then made a sharp right turn and headed down a hill. They had continued for about a half-mile when they spotted the entrance to the mine. It was carved into the side of the mountain. Both Christian and Winger were surprised at the amount of activity around the mine entrance. There were children and drones all around, very busy, pushing small carts that carried dirt from the bowels of the mine. They were dumping the dirt and returning to the mine all the while under the watchful eyes of the drones. The procession seemed endless. As children went back into the mine pushing their carts others were coming out.

They looked around to see if they could spot any of Mustgreed's soldiers but didn't see any.

"Let's climb this hill behind the mine and see if their camp is up there," Winger pointed.

"Good idea," Christian answered as he started up the hill making sure he was still under the protection of the dark forest.

They were about halfway up the hill when they heard the alarm from the camp below. It sounded like it was coming from an area between them and the mess hall where they had come from earlier.

Christian and Winger looked down toward where the alarm was coming from. It was difficult to make out what was going on and still remain in the dark forest. Just then, they heard the galloping of horses and saw four soldiers on horseback heading down the hill towards the area where the sound of the alarm was coming from. The soldiers looked tough and had many weapons strapped to their sides and some in the holsters of their saddles. After the soldiers passed the area where Christian and Winger were, they decided to come out of the dark forest long enough to take a quick look to see what was going on.

What they saw saddened their hearts. Around the area of the mess hall, a drone had a child by the arm. The child was putting up a fierce struggle until two more drones came to the assistance of the first.

"Do you know who that is?" Winger asked.

"I think so," Christian responded with obvious concern in his voice.

"Yes," Winger responded. "It's Tom."

Chapter 33

Tom had decided that he would wait to see what Christian and Winger were going to do even though he knew that he shouldn't. He thought to himself that he would surprise them when they returned to the spot where they left him. As he hung around he became very bored. The smells of the food cooking in the mess hall started to make him hungry. He knew that the food that was cooking was not very good, nevertheless, the aroma was getting to him. He decided to sneak up to the mess hall and take a look around and maybe, just maybe, he could get some food. He figured that even if he were spotted, he could run back into the dark forest because the drones weren't fast enough to catch him. They would never enter the dark forest.

He cautiously came out of the dark forest and keeping low, crawled to the mess hall window to peek in. There was not much going on inside. Some children were doing dishes, and a drone was at the far end of the mess hall, sitting on a chair that was tilted against the wall as he dozed. Then he spotted it! There were some sandwiches sitting on a table close to the door. Although he knew better, he decided to get one. He slowly went to the door and opened it as quietly as possible. He entered the mess hall keeping his eye on the drone who was snoozing at the opposite end of the building. Tom's confidence soared thinking that even if the drone woke up, he could outrun him to the dark forest where the drone would never enter, and he would be safe. First he took one sandwich, then decided to take several, stuffing them in his pockets. *This was so very easy,* he thought to himself. He started to back out the door, and he looked around. No one saw him. He smiled to himself as he closed the door behind him. Then, he turned to head back to the dark forest and spotted another drone for the first time.

The drone was headed toward the mess hall door when he spotted Tom. Tom made the mistake of thinking he could run past the drone and with his superior speed get into the dark forest before the drone realized what had happened. Unfortunately for Tom, the drone swiftly reached out just far enough to catch Tom's shirt and held onto it thereby stopping Tom's forward motion. The drone then grabbed Tom's arm and no matter how hard Tom struggled, he could not break his grasp. The drone then blew his whistle, and the alarms were sounded throughout the camp. Other drones immediately came to the first drone's assistance, and Tom realized he was captured, and there was nothing he could do.

Within minutes, four of Mustgreed's soldiers had arrived. One of them snarled at Tom, "What are you doing here? What barracks do you belong to?"

Thinking fast, Tom gave him the barracks number that he belonged to before his escape.

"How come your not in the mine working?" the soldier asked.

"I was so hungry I couldn't work," Tom lied hoping the soldiers and the drones wouldn't catch on. "I hid under my bed, and then after everyone left, I came to the mess hall to get some food." The soldier looked at Tom, and then without warning smacked him hard across the face.

"That will teach you," the soldier said. Then, turning to the drones, he ordered two of them to take Tom to the mine.

"If you ever try that again," the soldier admonished, "I'll throw you into the dark forest."

Tom rubbed his sore face where the soldier had struck him and thought to himself, *that he wished they would throw him back into the dark forest.*

The soldiers got back up on their horses and started back down the hill. Tom, with a drone on each side of him, was unceremoniously dragged in the direction of the mine.

Christian and Winger ducked back into the forest as the soldiers, who were riding their horses, came back towards them. After the soldiers passed, they looked out again from the edge of the forest in an attempt to see what was happening to Tom.

"At least the soldiers didn't take him," Winger observed.

"Yes, but look, the drones are bringing him in this direction," Christian answered.

"What shall we do? Do you think we should reveal ourselves and rescue him?" Winger asked pensively.

"I guess we can't let them take him. Here's what we'll do. When they get close, we'll jump out of the forest, and if the drones won't give him up without a fight, or if they give us a hard time, we'll just have to take them out," Christian said.

The drones, unknowingly, were about one hundred and fifty yards from where Christian and Winger were hidden. They were walking on each side of Tom when Tom realized he had an opportunity to escape. Each of the drones thought that the other was holding Tom's arm, when in fact, neither one of them held Tom. As soon as he felt the drones were relaxed enough, Tom bolted forward and ran full speed towards the forest. The drones, startled by this unexpected development, hesitated a second, long enough for Tom to get away. Tom knew that once he was out of their reach and running full speed, the drones would never be able to keep up. Once again the whistles and then the alarm was sounded, but this time, Tom was far enough away and soon went crashing into the forest. The drones lumbered their way to the edge of the forest and then stopped. They looked at each other and just stood there with their hands on their hips, not knowing what to do.

Christian and Winger were almost caught off guard. They were watching what was going on with Tom and the drones when the soldiers on horseback, once again, came riding in their direction and almost spotted them. They both quickly leapt back into the dark forest just before the soldiers got to them. After the soldiers passed, Christian and Winger came back into the clearing to get a better view of what was happening. When the soldiers arrived at the location where the drones were standing, it was obvious that heated words were being exchanged between them.

Christian and Winger decided that they would head back into the forest towards where Tom had fled. They wanted to get there as soon as possible in case the soldiers entered the forest in pursuit of Tom. They still did not know if the soldiers had a fear of the forest or not.

They moved as quickly as they could, however, the thick foliage of the forest made it difficult to make any rapid headway. When they got to the area near where the drones and the soldiers had been arguing, they cautiously peered out into the clearing to see what was going on. There were only two soldiers and the two drones there.

"Do you think the other two soldiers are in the forest going after Tom?" Winger whispered to Christian.

"Probably," Christian answered. "We'd better hurry," he added.

They moved as quickly as the forest would permit while trying to be as quiet as possible. Before long, they saw the two soldiers coming in their direction. Christian and Winger ducked into some heavy underbrush until the soldiers passed them by. Before long, the soldiers were back on their mounts and heading back down the hill, and the drones were slowly walking towards the mess hall.

Christian and Winger waited until the drones and soldiers were out of sight.

"You don't suppose they killed Tom and left him in the woods somewhere, do you?" Winger asked with fear in his voice.

"I don't think so," Christian responded. "I think they would have captured him and brought him back to the drones."

"I hope you're right, but where is he?" Winger asked, looking around with his sharp owl eyes.

"I don't know. Let's continue down the path, hopefully we'll catch up to him," Christian said.

They kept walking and walking until they were at the location where they originally left Tom, near the mess hall. To their disappointment, Tom wasn't anywhere to be seen. It was getting late, so they decided to head back to the cave. They were sure that Tom had beaten a rapid retreat and would be waiting for them with his friends in the cave.

When they arrived at the cave, as usual, the log was lifted and they entered. The children gathered about them with puzzled looks on their faces. Then they all asked the same question, "Where is Tom?" Christian and Winger's heart sank as they realized that Tom, indeed, had not returned to the cave.

Chapter 34

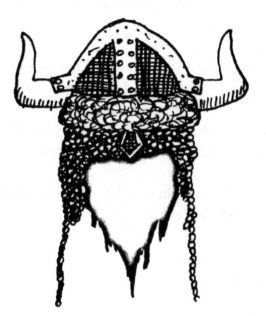

It was getting dark out, and Christian and Winger were worried. There still was no sign of Tom.

"Let's get back out there and look for him," Christian said.

"No," Winger responded. "It's dark, and you won't be able to see anything. No sense you getting lost too. I'll go by myself. Don't forget I can see at night."

"I want to come," Christian answered.

"No, you'll just hold me up. I won't be able to travel as fast with you, and besides, you should stay back and get some rest and make plans for the rescue of the children," Winger said, his voice full of confidence.

"I know you're right," Christian said, "but I just don't like the idea of sending you out at night in the dark forest all alone and without me."

"The main thing is to find Tom. I'll double back up the path where we traveled today. I'm sure I can find him if he is okay. Besides, the forest is safer for me at night than it is during the day," Winger said as he made his way to the front of the cave.

As much as he wanted to go, Christian realized that what Winger said made sense, and he reluctantly let Winger go out into the dark forest by himself.

Even though Winger could see in the darkness of the forest, it was still very slow going on account of the heavy foliage. He trudged his way to the area by the mess hall where they left Tom earlier that day. Tom was nowhere to be seen.

Winger decided he would try to call Tom in a voice loud enough to carry but not loud enough for anyone in the barracks to hear.

He placed his open hand on the right side of his mouth, the side which the barracks was on, in an attempt to block the sound on that side as much as possible.

"Tom.....Tom," he called half whispering and yet trying to project his voice as far as possible.

There was no response.

"Tom.....Tom," he tried again, but still no answer.

Tom was shivering, half from the cold and half from his close encounter with Mustgreed's soldiers. They had surprised him when they followed him into the forest after he got away from the drones. He had hidden under some thick bushes, and they went right by him without seeing him. That was one time he was happy to be in the dark forest. *Oh well,* he thought, *at least now they knew that the soldiers were not afraid of the forest the way that the drones were.* This was going to make things very difficult for all the children he thought. They would no longer be safe in the cave if the soldiers ever followed them, or for that matter, just followed the trails he, Christian and Winger naturally made just by walking through the forest. He knew he had to get back to warn all of them. He also knew that there was no way he could do it until daylight. It was very dark in the forest, and he knew there was no way he could ever find his way back to the cave. Tom knew he would have to make the best of it until morning. He began to make himself a bed of leaves, when he thought he heard someone calling his name. *Impossible,* he thought to himself. *It can't be.* He listened intently but didn't hear it again. *I guess it's my imagination playing tricks on me,* he thought. He completed his makeshift bed and lay down and covered himself with leaves and waited for sleep to overtake him.

Winger walked along the path looking from side to side, straining his eyes, in an attempt to see in the thick foliage. He realized he wasn't making much headway and had to come up with a better idea.

He thought that if he went into the clearing under the cover of darkness he could take flight and look for Tom from the vantage point high above the camp just in case Tom was in the clearing or looking up from where ever he was.

Winger quietly moved to the clearing by the mess hall. After entering it, he attempted to take flight, however, he had forgotten how badly burnt he was from his battle with the dragon. Trying as hard as he could, Winger could only lift himself a few feet off the ground. After several tries, he landed back on the ground, exhausted from the fruitless attempts. He sat there for several moments catching his breath and resting. When he felt he had his strength back, he reentered the forest and decided to continue down the path they had taken earlier in the day.

The drone was sitting in the kitchen on a chair staring off into space. Suddenly his attention was drawn to a noise coming from outside the rear door area. He listened intently. There it was again. It sounded like wings flapping in the air. He stiffened in his chair and sat bolt-upright. Again he heard the noise. He decided to investigate and slowly made his way towards the back door. The lights in the kitchen were out, but he knew his way around even in the dark. He had worked in the kitchen for the past five years and was familiar with every nook and cranny. When he got to the door, he opened it a crack and peeked out. Much to his amazement, he saw a huge bird flopping up and down. The bird finally stopped and was sitting on the ground no more than twenty yards from him. The drone picked up a frying pan and slowly started creeping towards the figure. He was only about five yards into his foray when the big bird got up like a man and walked into the dark forest. The drone was stupefied! He rubbed his eyes and questioned if he actually saw a human- bird. *Anything is possible from the dark forest*, he thought. He decided not to tell the others because they would only make fun of him. He wasn't sure himself if he actually had seen anything. *Ah*, he thought to himself, *it probably was just a shadow, or was it???*

Winger continued on, unaware of the drone and potential disaster that almost struck him. He walked further up the path and decided to try to call out for Tom again. Tom...Tom. He listened nothing.

The drone almost fell off the chair. He had just sat down again when he heard the calls. He hastily went back to the door and peered out. As usual, he saw nothing but darkness. *This time I know I heard something,* he said to himself. But he saw nothing. He thought to himself, *should I sound the alarm? But there is nothing there. It was probably just an animal, but it did sound like a human. Maybe it was the birdman.* He decided to stay by the door and listen and look, and if he saw or heard anything else he would send the alarm.

Winger continued on the path. It seemed much harder to travel at night even with his owl eyes. After a while, he stopped again and called out, "Tom....Tom."

"Over here," was the unexpected response.

"I'm over here," Tom said after he recognized Winger's voice.

"Keep talking so I can follow your voice," a relieved Winger answered.

"Am I glad to hear your voice! I thought I would be stuck here all night," Tom said as he heard the rustle of leaves and bushes as Winger came closer.

When they came together, Tom gushed out his story about how Mustgreed's soldiers followed him into the forest and almost captured him and how now they must be very careful because they don't have a fear of the dark forest that the drones have.

When Tom calmed down, Winger slowly led him back down the path towards the direction of the cave and the others.

Tom kept talking out of nervousness. He was anxious because of the events of the day and because he was walking in the sheer blackness of the forest at night.

As they passed near the area of the kitchen, the drone heard it again. This time there was no mistaking it! It was voices and they were coming from an area in the dark forest near the rear of the kitchen. He immediately sounded the alarm.

Lights went on all over the camp. Drones came out of different buildings wiping the sleep from their eyes and looking around in a daze. Almost immediately, the sound of galloping horses could be heard in the distance as the soldiers came towards the kitchen and the sound of the alarm. Even the children peered out of the few windows in their barrack like hovels, everyone straining their eyes to try to see what was happening.

Winger and Tom stopped in their tracks when they heard the alarm. There was no mistaking the sound of the horses as they approached. Winger peered out into the clearing and saw the soldiers coming fast carrying torches of fire to light their way. It was a very eerie sight.

"What shall we do?" Tom asked.

"Get behind me Tom," Winger said as he drew his sword from its scabbard. "If they come in after us, we'll have to fight. We're close to the cave, and I don't want them to follow us there. We'll back up into the forest a little more and hide behind the thicket, but if they see us we'll fight.

The soldiers arrived at the rear of the kitchen and began to question the drone who had sounded the alarm. It was clear that the soldiers were annoyed and only half-heartedly believed the drone.
Winger could see the drone motioning towards the dark forest where he and Tom stood. He grabbed Tom with his hand and took him further into the forest but not on the path.

"Stay here," Winger said.

Before Tom could answer, Winger disappeared into the black night.

He went back to the path and hurriedly tried to cover both the path leading to the cave and the fresh path he and Tom had just made. As he worked, he could see the lights of the torches coming in his direction. He stopped his work and backed to the location where he left Tom, trying to cover his tracks as he moved.

The soldiers entered the dark forest. Winger counted three torches. It could mean that there were only three of them, or some did not carry the torches. He hoped for the former.

The soldiers, upon entering the forest, separated and lackadaisically beat the bushes with their swords with one hand and extended the torches with the other, trying to see in the black, ominous forest.

One of the soldiers came in the direction of Winger and Tom. He was whacking at the bushes and coming directly at them. When he got very close, Tom moved to get out of the rays of the light the torch was throwing, but the movement made noise and attracted the attention of the soldier. The soldier lifted the torch higher in order to cast a longer light in the direction of the noise. Then he saw them, a boy and a birdman. *The drone wasn't crazy after all*, he thought to himself. He pointed his sword towards them and said with a sneer on his face, "Get up and come here." Winger got up, and then the soldier spotted his sword and told him to drop it, but Winger had different ideas. He thrust his sword at the soldier who immediately parried and warded off the blow. The soldier then let out a yell, and Tom could see the other torches making their way towards them as Winger and the soldier fought.

It's the end, Tom thought. *They're going to kill us!* The other soldiers were getting closer and closer.

Winger and the soldier fought fiercely. It was obvious that Winger was the stronger and more skilled with the sword. The soldier kept backing away from Winger's thrusts and swings of his sword. The problem was that if the other soldiers joined the battle, he probably wouldn't stand a chance against all three.

163

Winger realized that the other soldiers were getting nearer and decided on his course of action. He backed up a bit and when the soldier advanced, Winger swung his sword at the torch the soldier was holding in his left hand. The torch was sliced in two with the flaming part falling to the ground on the path between themselves and the other approaching soldiers. The tinder dry leaves immediately ignited, and the fire caused the approaching soldiers, who were almost next to their compatriot by this time, to stop and back away. Then, the soldier who was fighting with Winger made a fatal mistake. Distracted by the fire, he took his eyes off Winger for a split second and glanced at what was now an inferno. This gave Winger the opening he was looking for, and he quickly thrust his sword into the soldier ending the brief but fierce struggle.

Without hesitation, Winger grabbed Tom's hand. Running as fast as he could through the woods, he literally dragged Tom behind him. As they ran, they could hear the commotion of the soldiers and additional alarms coming from the clearing.

At last they arrived at the cave. Christian, who couldn't sleep, was waiting just inside the entrance of the cave. He heard noises and knew someone was coming. As soon as he was sure it was Winger and Tom, he lifted the log for them to enter.

Everyone inside jumped up and was elated to see that Tom had been found. Christian, however, didn't like the look on Winger's face and realized that something was wrong. Winger and Tom quickly explained what had happened. Looking out the cave entrance, they could see the flames which by this time were enormous and lighting up the sky. There was no doubt, the fire was getting bigger and heading in their direction.

"No time for talk now," Christian said. "Grab everything you can, and let's get out of here."

"How can we, it pitch black out there?" Peggy said motioning towards the forest.

"I'll take the lead, and everyone will hold the hand of the person behind them," Winger said.

"I think it's our only chance. If the flames don't engulf the cave, Mustgreed's soldiers will probably be right behind, and with no foliage to hide us, they're sure to find us," Christian added.

They quickly bundled up everything they could, mainly pots and pans and the odds and ends each child had. Winger and Christian put on their armor and also put the armor on the horses. Before long, they were ready. They lifted the log and a long line started with Winger at the lead and each child following in a single file. Christian brought up the rear making sure no one was lost.

It was very dark in the forest, and the children were scared. Every crack of a branch or every time one of them would have an unseen leaf touch their face, it would cause them to let out a yelp. Winger and Christian kept talking back and forth to try to reassure the children that all was well.

They came to the clearing they had used for their rest area during the battle with the dragon and decided to stop for a while. The clearing had some light, thanks to the full moon. Christian did not want to start a fire for fear that Mustgreed's soldiers might be on their trail.

The children all huddled together while Christian and Winger tried to figure out their next move. The flames that they could see did not look as if they were heading in their direction, so they knew they had some time to formulate a plan. They decided they couldn't go back to the cave in the event Mustgreed's soldiers found it. It wouldn't take them long to realize what it was, and they probably would set up a trap waiting for them to return. They decided to forge ahead with their rescue of the children and came up with a plan that just might make due with a lot of work and luck.

They told the children their plan. The children loved it because it included them. Christian warned them that if it didn't work it would probably mean that they would end up in captivity again and at the mercy of Mustgreed and his soldiers and drones. The children were excited and felt that it would work and were very willing to chance it.

"After all," Tom said, "what else can we do? Without the cave and Christian and Winger, there is no hope. I'll take my chances," he said to the other children.

They all agreed.

"Okay, let's rest here, and at first daylight we'll head for the camp," Christian said.

Dawn came quickly. The excitement of the night robbed most of the children of sleep. The children shared what little food they had taken with them and foraged the nearby forest for fruit and berries.

Soon it was time to leave.

Christian led the way. First, he headed for the area where the dragon had been slain and then made a sharp turn to the right heading for the clearing. It was rough going, and Christian had to hack his way using his sharp sword. He figured it should lead them to the camp midway between the dining hall and the mines. He wanted to be at about where Tom had run into the forest in his escape from the drones. He figured this would put them at an advantage of being far enough away from the drones at the barracks and within minutes of Mustgreed's soldiers.

At last, they arrived at the camp. They all remained quiet as Christian peered into the clearing. All seemed normal. From where they were they could not see the area where Winger fought the soldier and where the fire was.

"Okay, it looks like its all clear," Christian said.

"Everyone get busy and start on the jobs we talked about last night," he continued. "If you have any questions, don't be afraid to ask. Everything must be perfect for this to work, and whatever you do, be as quiet as possible. Marie, you stand guard at the clearing, and if you see anyone, let us know immediately, and then everyone will stop work and be quiet."

The children immediately busied themselves performing the tasks they had been assigned. Some went with Winger to gather vines, while others worked about five feet in from the clearing.

Several times during the day work had to stop because soldiers on horseback passed. The interruptions were brief and didn't interfere with the work that much. When late afternoon came, Christian and Winger decided that it was getting too late to continue. They went back about a hundred yards from the clearing and started to make a camp by clearing the brush with their swords. When they felt it was large enough, they had all the children stop work and settle down into their makeshift camp.

Winger and a few of the children then foraged near the campsite to gather whatever food was available. There wasn't enough to satisfy all the children, so Winger headed down the path that they made on the previous day. He decided to raid the mess hall. When he came to where the fire had burnt all the foliage near the mess hall, he told the children that were with him to wait until he gave them the all clear sign.

Winger cautiously looked around and seeing no one, ran into the clearing and then into the mess hall. There were two drones inside lounging around waiting for the children to arrive from the mines for dinner. There were also several children working hard setting the tables. Winger drew his sword and motioned for the two frightened drones to move to where there were two chairs. The children stood motionless not knowing what to make of this birdman who invaded the mess hall. Winger motioned with his sword for the drones to sit down. Then he motioned the children who were waiting in the woods to come ahead.

When they arrived, the children in the mess hall greeted them. Most of them knew each other. Winger tied the drones to the chairs using some vines he had brought with him. He then told all the children, those who were with him and those who were in the mess hall, to gather as much food as possible and place it in pots. He took as many of the metal utensils as they could carry. He then told the children to go back into the woods. At first, the children from the mess hall did not want to go into the dark forest, but with the assurances from the other children, they went.

Winger kept stopping on the way back to their temporary campsite to cover their trail. They made it back just before night. The children in the campsite were surprised to see those from the mess hall and in their excitement, raised their voices. Christian had to calm them down for fear that they would be heard.

During the night, the sounds of horses could be heard coming from down the hill and going towards the mess hall. Twice Christian and Winger went to the clearing to see what was happening. It was the soldiers on horses carrying torches and probably looking for a birdman and some children.

The next morning, they woke up as soon as some sun could be seen through the thick canopy of the dark forest. They ate whatever food was left and made their way to the edge of the clearing. Christian and Winger were in full-battle regalia and so were their horses. After checking on the last minute preparations the children had made, Christian fashioned a pole out of a small branch from a tree and fastened a white rag on it. Then he and Winger rode out on their stallions into the clearing to await their fate.

It didn't take long. Alarms were sounded all over the camp and within minutes, the sounds of soldiers on horseback came from the top of the hill. Christian and Winger braced themselves. Four soldiers on horseback came within eyesight of them and stopped. Then one left and went back. Before long, Christian and Winger saw what looked to be sixty or seventy horsemen heading their way, and at the lead was a huge soldier who was dressed like Attila the Hun. He had a helmet on his head with horns coming out each side. He looked very mean. Even his leather garments lent themselves to his fierce-looking demeanor.

Christian looked at Winger and said, "Well this is it old friend." "I guess so," Winger answered as the soldiers came closer and closer.

They both took a deep breath and slowly headed toward the oncoming army.

Chapter 35

The army drew nearer.

Christian waved the makeshift white flag.

Then Mustgreed raised his hand, and the small army stopped about fifty yards in front of them. Mustgreed turned and spoke to some of the riders near him. They were too far for Christian and Winger to hear anything. Then the four riders galloped to where Christian and Winger were.

"The exalted leader of the universe, his Excellency, Mustgreed, wants to know who you are and what are you doing here. Why should he not cut you to ribbons and leave you as scraps for the dogs?" one the riders asked. They couldn't take their eyes off Winger, obviously stunned at this half-bird and half-man.

"I am Sir Knight and this is Winger," Christian said. "We have come here as an advanced party of the mighty King Baltimore, who at this very minute is advancing with an army of five thousand men," Christian bluffed, hoping he was believable.

The soldiers looked at each other, obviously worried.

"What does King Baltimore want from us?" was their response.

"One of the children you are holding is his nephew, so he has decided to free all the children and take all who are responsible and make them pay for their crimes," Christian responded.

Once again, the soldiers looked at each other in disbelief.

"How did you get past the dragon?" the soldiers inquired.

"The noble King has many weapons," Christian responded. "We killed him with a catapult," he continued. "It wasn't at all difficult for a King who has defeated most of the armies of the world."

"What do you want of us?" the soldier said, a nervous pitch in his voice revealing his anxiety.

172

Christian raised the flag twice in succession, and the children rattled the pots and pans and pulled on vines which they had worked on the day before. This action made the bushes at the edge of the forest shake for about fifty yards across.

The soldiers looked towards the forest and sweat broke on their foreheads.

"See, the archers are already setting up for their deadly fire," Christian said.

"Tell the soldiers that the noble King Baltimore has no quarrel with them, and if they leave peaceably he will not pursue them. As for Mustgreed, he will accompany us back to the King's royal tent to have judgment passed upon him for his despicable acts. Now go and tell him everything we said and make it quick before our patience with you runs out and we darken the sky with our arrows," Christian said.

The soldiers turned their horses around and headed back to Mustgreed.

As the soldiers approached, Mustgreed could see the look of concern on their faces.

"What do those two want?" Mustgreed asked.

"They are emissaries of King Baltimore," the soldiers responded. "They want the children released. One of them is his nephew. They killed the dragon and have an army of five thousand knights coming. The forest is filled with them. I saw them with my own eyes." Mustgreed looked at the other three soldiers who had accompanied him, and they all chimed in by saying it was true. The edge of the forest is full of archers who have us in their sights.

"They promised not to hurt us if we leave, but they want to take you to see the king," the soldiers continued.

When this was heard by some of the soldiers nearby, it quickly spread through the ranks of Mustgreed's army. The men began talking among themselves. It was clear that they wanted to leave. After all, they rationalized, they were not responsible for what Mustgreed made them do. Why stay here and die for something we did not do?

Mustgreed could sense what was being said and the rebellion that was fostering within the ranks of the soldiers.

"I will show these insolent devils that they cannot mess with Mustgreed," he shouted out loud.

"Who is with me?" he shouted, as he took out his sword and raised it high in an attempt to rally his men behind him.

The hesitation on the part of most of his men was obvious to all.

"Are you all cowards?" Mustgreed yelled. "Let us show them that we are not afraid to die. Now who is with me?"

He rode his horse forward several feet, then stopped to see who was following. His soldiers were still hesitant.

He tried his final play. He stood high on his horse and waved his sword and shouted, "Charge".

As his horse started galloping towards Christian and Winger, he turned his head and saw that only four soldiers, his personal guards, stayed with him.

The children at the edge of the forest were intently watching what was happening in the clearing.

At Christians signal, they busily went about their duties of making just enough noise to be subtle but to get the message across that there were many people at the edge of the forest.

"It's working," Tom said excitedly, as he watched the four soldiers turn to look at where the noise was coming from.
Then they saw the soldiers had listened to what Christian had told them. They rode back to where Mustgreed was waiting.

"If they didn't believe them, they would have attacked by now," Tom observed.

"I don't know," Sue answered. "I wish we could hear what they're saying."

The children's hearts sank as they saw Mustgreed draw his sword and swing it high in the air while shouting at his men.

Then Mustgreed started galloping towards Christian and Winger.

"Shouldn't we run deeper into the forest?" a nervous Marie asked.

None of the children answered her. They were too busy watching what was happening in the clearing.

"Only five coming our way," Winger said drawing his sword.

"Yes, but if the others remain there and do not see any knights coming from the forest to assist us, they will realize it was a bluff and join the attack," Christian answered.

"I don't think it will make much of a difference anyway. Five to two are pretty big odds," Winger responded.

Christian dropped the flag and drew his sword.
The two valiant knights charged at the oncoming Mustgreed and his soldiers.

As the distance between them became shorter and shorter, Christian looked up and saw the remainder of Mustgreed's army was still sitting there watching what was happening.

"I'll take the three on the left, you can take Mustgreed and the one on the right," Winger yelled above the noise of the galloping horses.

"Okay," Christian yelled back.

"Come on move away," Christian muttered to himself looking at the soldiers who remained behind.

Then the first blow from Mustgreed struck Christian's shield as the combatants galloped passed each other. He quickly ducked under the blow aimed at his head from the second soldier as he passed. Then they turned their horses in order to attack each other again.

Winger kept his sharp owl eyes on the three soldiers attacking him. They came at him at furious speed three abreast. Winger, waiting for the last possible second, turned his galloping horse sharply to the left and by doing so, two of his foes could not get a swing at him. He swung his sword at the soldier nearest him, smashed it into the shield of the soldier and deflected the soldier's sword with his own shield. Meanwhile, the other two who were left out of the fray because of Winger's maneuver, cussed and started to turn their horses around to get another try at Winger.

When the soldiers who were watching the battle saw no one coming to Christian and Wingers aid, they started to trot towards them.

Christian and Winger realized that they would never be able to handle the onslaught of the impending doom about to be foisted upon them by Mustgreed's army who were, by this time, rapidly approaching.

Chapter 36

Christian and Winger were fighting valiantly. Swords could be seen flashing as they caught the rays of the sun. The clanging of sword against shield could be heard throughout the valley.

Mustgreed's army was getting closer. *We're finished,* Winger thought to himself.

The children watched the impending disaster with fear in their hearts. The army would capture or kill Christian and Winger and then come after them.

Tom sprung to his feet.

"We can't just stand by and do nothing," he shouted at the children.

"Grab the vines, let's start making noise, maybe they'll think the knights have arrived."

With that order the children seemed to snap out of their sense of frustration and started yelling in as deep a voice as they could muster. They pulled on the vines and shook the bushes and banged on pots and pans.

The soldiers had taken out their swords and began picking up speed heading towards the combatants. Their eyes, however, were fixed on the forest for fear that arrows would start flying in their direction. Just then, all kinds of commotion started at the edge of the forest. A soldier who was in the lead put his shield above his head to protect himself from the certainty of incoming arrows. The other soldiers seeing this, immediately followed suit and raised their shields over their heads. Then, they turned and fled as fast as their horses could take them away from the fight. They fled in fear and vowed to themselves that they would never return to Mustgreed and this prison camp.

Soon they were out of sight.

The distraction of the noise coming from the forest caused one of the soldiers Winger was fighting to look towards the forest and proved fatal. Winger was able to slash him under his vest armor almost severing him in two.

The battle was a demanding struggle for both Christian and

Winger. Fighting on horseback and against two opponents was extremely difficult. The soldiers would come at Christian and Winger, one from either side. They would have to ward off a blow from one of the soldier's swords with their shield, while using their sword to fight the other opponent.

One of the soldiers, who was fighting against Winger, charged at him, jumped off his horse and grabbed Winger's shield causing him to fall off his horse and onto the ground. Winger immediately got to his feet as did his opponent. In the meantime, the other soldier, remaining on the horse, charged at Winger swinging his sword at him. Winger side-stepped the potentially fatal blow as he swung his sword at the soldier who was on the ground with him and missed. The soldier engaged Winger with a series of quick sword blows which Winger deflected with his shield. Then, the soldier on horseback charged again and from his height reined several more blows at Winger who was rapidly being force backwards. It looked like Winger was a goner, barely able to defend himself from the blows of the soldier on the ground and from those coming from the soldier above. Winger then called up all his strength and power and immediately took flight. Due to his burnt wings, he was only able to hover about six-feet above the horseman, but that was enough. All the soldiers and Mustgreed were shocked at this development. Winger then came down and dive bombed the soldier on the ground sending his sword into his shoulder. The soldier on horseback, observing this development, immediately spurred his horse and took off, running away. He was quickly followed by the soldier who was fighting with Christian leaving Mustgreed alone.

When Mustgreed realized that he was alone, he immediately spurred his horse and galloped away in the direction his men had taken. Christian took off after him.

Winger could not follow immediately because he had to retrieve his horse.

They galloped for miles until Christian caught up with Mustgreed. Mustgreed, seeing that Christian was alone, turned his horse in a circle and swung his sword at Christian, who deflected the blow with his shield. The two, each astride their horses, swung blow after blow at each other. Each time, their opponent deflected the blows. At times, the combatants were so close that they could smell each other's breath. Then, Mustgreed got lucky. One of his deflected blows glanced off Christian's shield and struck his sword hand causing him to drop it. Mustgreed, spurred on by this lucky break, continued to rain blows at Christian who was warding them off with his shield. Christian reached to his belt and pulled out his knife, but it wasn't even a tenth of the size of Mustgreed's unforgiving sword. Christian had to do something fast, or eventually Mustgreed would beat him down with his unanswered sword blows. Christian timed the next blow and leapt at Mustgreed's horse's head. He twisted its head causing the startled horse to fall on its side, unceremoniously dumping it's rider to the ground. Christian scrambled along the ground trying to get to his sword. Mustgreed attacked! He plunged his sword at Christian, who was lying on the ground. Christian quickly moved his body sideways avoiding the sword strike by less than an inch. Mustgreed was leaning over Christian with his sword in the ground almost up to its hilt. Then it happened!

Mustgreed's forward motion made him fall onto Christian's knife which he was holding in front of him. Mustgreed tried to continue the battle, but it was no use. The stab wound was fatal.

Just then, Winger rode up and immediately got off his horse to assist Christian, but it was not necessary. Christian was lying under Mustgreed and struggling to get the weight of his dead foe off of him.

"Are you going to help me, or just stand there gawking?" Christian said to his grinning friend.

Winger walked over and pulled Mustgreed's limp body off Christian.

"I guess that does it. I don't see any of his soldiers, so I think that does it for Mustgreed and Company," Winger said still grinning as he looked around.

"I sure hope so," Christian responded. "I'm bone-weary tired, but we'd better get back and make sure the children are alright."

They mounted up and galloped back to where they left the children. When they arrived they were in for a surprised ...The children were gone!

Chapter 37

Christian and Winger looked at each other. Each had a puzzled look on their face.

"What could have happened to them?" Winger asked.

"I don't know, maybe they went back into the forest for some reason, or maybe they're trying to rescue the other children," Christian responded.

Just then, they spotted some of the drones running from the area of the mess hall. Christian and Winger smiled at each other.

"Of course, they were hungry," Winger laughed.

They started their horses towards the mess hall, and as they approached, the drones were running towards them and away from the mess hall.

"Please sir, don't hurt us, we were only following Mustgreed's orders. If we didn't do what he told us, he was going to throw us into the dark forest to be eaten by the dragon," one of the frightened drones said to Christian.

"Very well, we will let you go this time, but if we ever hear that you are doing this kind of work again, we won't be so easy on you the next time," Christian replied.

"Oh thank you, thank you sir," the drone responded.

"Now, I want you to go throughout the camp and tell all the children to come to the mess hall, and be quick about it," Christian said. "If you do a good job and bring all the children to the mess hall, I will let all the drones go free," Christian continued.

"Yes sir, yes sir," the drones repeated and took off in different directions in their quest to gather the children.

Christian and Winger rode towards the mess hall. When they arrived and entered, they saw the missing children. They were renewing old acquaintances with the other children who had been prisoners until they arrived a few minutes ago and chased the drones out.

Tom and some of the others were busily eating and talking at the same time. It was a funny sight. It looked like an old school reunion.

"Listen up," Christian shouted to try to get everyone's attention.

"The other children will be arriving soon, so we are going to have some logistics problems to work out," Christian continued.

"I want all those who cooked in the mess hall to continue fixing meals for everyone. Tom, I want you and some of the children to start looking around and see what provisions we have. We're going to need to pack plenty of food for our trip back through the forest," Christian continued.

Some of the children started to busy themselves with their kitchen chores. This time they did the chores happily, and they had plenty of help from the other children who had volunteered. It was no longer a forced labor but a labor of love.

Christian and Winger immediately started to plan the trip back. They decided that they would have to gather all the children and get an idea of how many there were. Then if all were healthy enough, they would start the trip tomorrow morning after everyone got enough rest. They realized that they couldn't wait much longer than that because the children would be very excited and wanting to get home as soon as possible.

While they were still making plans, the drones arrived with the rest of the children. It was pandemonium in the mess hall. Shouts of greetings and hugs and crying broke out everywhere.

It took hours to get all the children quiet and to start organizing things. They counted one-hundred and forty-two children. Many of them had been in the camp for over a year and were very anxious to leave.

Christian and Winger decided to send all the children back to their barracks after they had finished eating their meals. As they ate, Christian told them about the dark forest and the trip that lay ahead of them. He instructed them to take very little as they would all have to carry food and other provisions for the trip. Christian then gave them instructions to meet back at the mess hall at sunrise in preparation for the trip back. The children couldn't believe that after all this time they were going home.

The next morning everyone met at the mess hall. Christian and Winger had already loaded their horses with as much supplies as they could carry. They made sleds of wood from the forest and attached them to the horses to drag behind them. When they were all loaded and the children had as much food as they could carry, they started their trek into the dark forest. Christian took the lead, hacking at the dense forest with his sword to widen the path. Winger brought up the rear, making sure that none of the children would fall behind. The children who had not previously been in the forest with Tom were at first very frightened as they approached the forest. However, when they saw that the others were going in and, with a little prodding from Winger, cautiously followed.

Christian tried to find the paths that they had originally made when they first entered the forest and before they met the dragon. He knew it was longer that way because they had to detour to the area of the cave and then to the path to the clearing near where the dragon was slain before they could find the path leading to the old churchyard, but he felt it was the safest route.

Before long, they passed the cave. The children, who had lived in the cave, explained the living conditions and the spiked log that guarded the entrance to the other children from the camp. Christian encouraged the talk figuring it would get the children's minds off the dark forest.

When they got to the rest area near where the dragon was slain, they decided to stop for the night. The children were given chores, mostly cooking and gathering loads of firewood for the night. Christian and Winger, using their swords, made the area larger in order to hold all the children. It was very hard work, clearing all the brush and small trees, but soon they were done and then sat and rested a while.

After of the children finished eating, they laid down to what Christian and Winger thought would be a quiet night. The fires were blazing, and there was plenty of firewood for the night. It was not to be. The children were too nervous. Tom and the other children, who were with him in the cave, told stories about the dragon and the beasts which made the children feel all the worse.

It went like this the next day. With each step, everyone could feel the excitement building as they thought about being home with their family and friends.

The next night, Christian and Winger were sitting around a nice, warm fire and relaxing. They thought about how lucky they were not to have run into any unexpected problems, especially with all the children. They had to admit that the children seemed to be able to take care of themselves. As they closed their eyes and slowly drifted off to sleep, they couldn't have any way of knowing what a horrible thing was waiting for them just a little further down the trail.

Chapter 38

They awoke in the morning feeling tired. Some of the children had nightmares during the night because of the stories the children told about the dragon and the beasts. They would let out yells which woke everyone up. Also, some of the other children were very excited about being so close to home that they, too, had a restless night.

After breakfast had been eaten, it was time to start out again down the path towards the village. Everyone was hoping that this would be the day that they would get out of the dark forest and be home again. Christian had calculated in his mind that they

189

should reach the village in four or five hours, but he wasn't sure. It was difficult to calculate anything in the forest. It was so dark and difficult to walk, and besides they made very slow headway because some of the children had difficulty keeping up. Winger, who was bringing up the rear, had to constantly urge the children to keep up the pace.

At last they passed the dark and slimy-looking swamp. The odor from it caused some of the children to gag. Christian calculated that they were about five hours to the village, based on his recollection of where the swamp was.

They had walked a little further when Christian heard screams coming from behind him. There was no doubt some of the children behind him were in trouble. Christian grabbed his shield from his horse and ran back to where the screams were coming from.

He didn't have to run far. There on the path in front of him was this terrifying-looking creature. It was about ten-feet long and looked like a large lizard except that it had large green scales on its sides. Its eyes were red just like those of the Dragon's offspring, but it was slithering on the ground on four little stubby legs. As it moved, it would stick out a long forked tongue and hiss at the children who were falling over each other in an attempt to get away from it. When it opened its mouth, it revealed double rows of sharp teeth with two large fangs which protruded from the upper jaw, overlapped the lower jaw and were always exposed and ready to kill its next meal.

When the creature saw Christian approach, it turned its ugly head towards him, and its tongue darted out at him. Christian was far enough away that the tongue didn't come close. By this time, Winger arrived from the other direction. He also had his sword and shield at the ready. The creature looked from Christian to Winger and kept darting out its tongue from one to the other.

"What shall we do?" asked Winger.

"I don't know," Christian responded.

"It isn't attacking us," Winger observed.

"Just the same, don't let down your guard...." Christian barely got the words out when the creature started to move in his direction, its tongue darting at him as it hissed.

Christian put his shield between himself and the creature. The creature's tongue struck the shield, and then suddenly its tail flailed up over its head and came right at Christian. That was the first time that Christian noticed the v-shaped spikes that were on the end of its tail. The spikes struck Christian's shield and dented it, and the force knocked Christian backwards onto the ground, his shield on top of him.

In the meantime, Winger observing the creature's thrust with its tail, decided to attack. He moved forward and swinging his sword, struck the creature's side. His sword bounced off the creature's scales which were like armor. The creature's tail then came back from its attack on Christian. Winger had to quickly sidestep to avoid being struck by it. After the tail hit the ground, the creature then swiftly moved it to the side hitting Winger in the legs and knocking him to the ground. Winger quickly balled himself up behind his shield as he lay on the ground and the creature's tail struck one blow after another.

Christian, seeing the predicament they were in, jumped to his feet. The creature seemed to have no problem attacking Winger with its murderous tail while its tongue continually darted at Christian, which was being deflected by his shield. At one point, the creature moved forward and attempted to bite Christian's shield. Christian hit it in the snout with his sword, but it seemed to have no effect on the creature at all. The creature again moved forward and let its tail arc over its head striking Christian's shield and knocking him to the ground with his shield on top of him. Then, the creature attempted to sink its huge fangs into Christian but again was thwarted by his shield.

When the creature attacked Christian with its tail, it gave Winger enough time to spring back onto his feet. As the tail came back towards him, he thrust his sword up to its hilt into the under part of the tail which did not have the protective scales. The huge stab wound did not seem to have any effect on the creature, and Winger almost lost his sword, having to pull it from the tail before it hit the ground.

Christian could tell by the sound of its hissing that the creature was getting very mad. Once again, it flicked its tongue at Christian, but this time Christian did not retreat. When the creature's tongue hit his shield, he swung his sword at it with all his might. The sword hit the creature's tongue, slicing a good two feet of its tip off. The piece of tongue fell to the ground.

Christian and the creature looked at it as it lay there. Then the creature turned and scurried back into the swamp and disappeared into the water leaving a trail of blood from its tail wound.

Christian and Winger looked at each other and then stared at where the creature disappeared.

"What was that?" Winger asked.

"I don't know, and I don't want to know," Christian responded.

"Let's get out of here," Winger continued. "I'll stay here until all the children pass. You'd better go ahead and take the lead again." Christian made his way to the front of the group and began leading the children forward at a slow pace allowing time for the others to catch up.

The children passed by Winger very slowly, staring out into the swamp, afraid that the creature might come out again.

Winger stayed at the area where they had just fought the creature until he was sure that all the children had passed that point and then took up his position at the rear of the column. He no longer had any problems with the children keeping up with the group; they moved away from the swamp as fast as they could.

At last, Christian came to the edge of the dark forest.

Chapter 39

As Winger stepped out of the dark forest and into the church's cemetery, he felt a great sense of relief. It was late afternoon and the shadows grew long as the sun was beginning to set. He stood there for a while and enjoyed the looks on the faces of the children's as they exited the forest. Their whole face would light up and express the joy and happiness they were feeling. They looked young again, probably for the first time in quite a while.

At last, Winger came out indicating that all the children were out of the forest. Christian had a big smile on his face. He walked over to Winger and threw his arms around him in a happy embrace. "There were times when I didn't think we'd make it," Christian said.

"I know. I felt the same way," Winger responded.

"Promise me that when this is over, you won't forget me," Winger asked.

"I promise," Christian said. "We are friends for life. After all, I do owe you my life. You saved me many times."

"And you saved me, so we're even," Winger said patting Christian on the back.

The Priest wondered what all the noise was in the cemetery. Could people be visiting this late in the afternoon? He looked out the window, and to his amazement, saw Christian and Winger and all the children. He immediately realized what had happened and that the children were saved. He shouted for the housekeeper to look. Then he ran into the church and immediately started to ring the church bells.

The people in the village stopped what they were doing and looked toward the direction of the church and wondered why the priest would be ringing the bells at this late hour. It must mean that he is in trouble or the church is on fire. They immediately headed toward the church to see if they could help.

The bells startled Christian and Winger as well as the children. "It's great to hear them," Winger said.

"It sure is," Christian agreed, as they walked toward the village.

It was a scene no one will ever forget. The people from the

195

village were heading toward the church, and the children were heading toward the village. All of a sudden everything in the entire world stopped. Parents realized their loved ones were home, and the children realized the dream that they dared not dream, for such a long time, finally came true. THEY WERE HOME!

Then all pandemonium broke loose. People were running everywhere. They were embracing each other and laughing, crying, hugging and kissing. They started dancing and throwing the little ones up in the air and catching them. It was the beginning of a party that would last all night in the village. There was music and singing and dancing until everyone was exhausted. That night, families who had been separated for such a long period of time slept under the same roof, and many children and parents had the first good night's sleep they had in a long time.

Christian and Winger stood back watching the entire scene with a sense of pride and accomplishment. Then they went back to the church and dropped to their knees and thanked God for bringing them through the horrible experiences of the dark forest and most of all, for bringing all the children back unharmed. They asked the Lord to never let anything like that happen again. While they were praying, they heard a loud crash outside. They rushed out and saw that the dark forest was on fire. It was burning brightly and at the rate the fire was spreading, it would consume the whole forest in no time.

"It was a miracle," the old priest said. "I never saw anything like it. A large lightning bolt came out of the sky and set the whole forest on fire."

Christian and Winger looked at each other and smiled.

* * * *

"Wake up, wake up, or you'll be late for school," Christian's mother said as she gently shook him.

Christian opened his eyes in disbelief.

"Where am I; what happened?" he asked.

"What a silly question, you're in your bed where you sleep every night," his mother responded.

"No I was in the dark forest with Winger, and we rescued the children," Christian responded.

"Oh no," his mother smiled. "You were right here in bed where you belong. I think you must have had a bad dream," his mother said, gently pushing the hair back from his brow.

"Now hurry up, get dressed and come downstairs for breakfast," she said as she left the room.

It can't be. It wasn't a dream. It was so real, Christian kept repeating over and over to himself as he got dressed.

Then he looked out the window and there it was. An owl was sitting on a branch of the tree in his yard.

"Winger," he called out.

The owl looked at him and attempted to fly, but it was having trouble. Its wing was burnt.

CPSIA information can be obtained at www.ICGtesting.com
Printed in the USA
LVOW04s1352090615

441753LV00002B/2/P